# RUBY & ROLAND

# RUBY & ROLAND

*A Novel*

# FAITH SULLIVAN

MILKWEED EDITIONS

The characters and events in this book are fictitious. Any similarity to real persons, living or dead, is coincidental and not intended by the author.

Published 2019 by Milkweed Editions
Printed in the United States of America
Cover design by Mary Austin Speaker
Cover art by Josef Wenig, from the bookplate of J. Čapek; image courtesy of the Pratt Institute Libraries—Ex Libris Collection.
19 20 21 22 23 5 4 3 2 1
*First Edition*

Milkweed Editions, an independent nonprofit publisher, gratefully acknowledges sustaining support from the Alan B. Slifka Foundation and its president, Riva Ariella Ritvo-Slifka; the Ballard Spahr Foundation; *Copper Nickel*; the Jerome Foundation; the McKnight Foundation; the National Endowment for the Arts; the National Poetry Series; the Target Foundation; and other generous contributions from foundations, corporations, and individuals. Also, this activity is made possible by the voters of Minnesota through a Minnesota State Arts Board Operating Support grant, thanks to a legislative appropriation from the arts and cultural heritage fund. For a full listing of Milkweed Editions supporters, please visit milkweed.org.

Library of Congress Cataloging-in-Publication Data

Names: Sullivan, Faith, author.
Title: Ruby and Roland : a novel / Faith Sullivan.
Description: First edition. | Minneapolis, Minnesota : Milkweed Editions, 2019.
Identifiers: LCCN 2019012601 (print) | LCCN 2019013533 (ebook) | ISBN 9781571319968 (ebook) | ISBN 9781571311320 (hardcover : alk. paper)
Classification: LCC PS3569.U3469 (ebook) | LCC PS3569.U3469 R83 2019 (print) | DDC 813/.54--dc23
LC record available at https://lccn.loc.gov/2019012601

Milkweed Editions is committed to ecological stewardship. We strive to align our book production practices with this principle, and to reduce the impact of our operations in the environment. We are a member of the Green Press Initiative, a nonprofit coalition of publishers, manufacturers, and authors working to protect the world's endangered forests and conserve natural resources. *Ruby & Roland* was printed on acid-free 30% postconsumer-waste paper by Sheridan Books, Inc.

*For Margaret and Davis, Jane, Sylvie, and new daughter Soomi.*

*And for my Wednesday Writers. If you didn't exist,*
*I'd have to invent you.*

When I am dead and opened,
you shall find Calais lying in my heart.

MARY I (1516-1558)

# RUBY & ROLAND

# CHAPTER ONE

I had a tiny red birthmark on my chest when I was born, a mark no bigger than the head of a pin on which ten thousand angels are said to dance. Serena, my mother, a woman of fanciful nature, declared it a ruby, hence my name. Denton, my father, felt it more resembled a radish. However, "radish" was thought an unsuitable name.

Serena was a teacher of grammar, locution, and literature at the public high school, Denton Drake an instructor of mathematics in the small normal school. When I was old enough, they saw to it that I read books, and Serena encouraged me to write little poems and essays. And, before that, when I was very small, Serena read lovely stories to me, stories about little girls in soft dresses who spread tea cloths in gazebos and poured pretend tea from china pots, or about other little girls who played with kittens under spreading plane trees while their nannies watched from nearby. I knew—and told Serena that I knew—that one day I would have a gazebo and a little girl of my own, and that for her fifth birthday I would buy her a china tea set. Then, on my sixth birthday, I woke to find at the foot of my bed a box with cellophane on the lid and, inside, a china tea set! On top was a note. "Happy Birthday, darling Ruby. Sorry there's no gazebo. Love, Serena and Denton."

Serena was endlessly clever. For instance, in our lunch pails (lidded, silver-colored lard pails, emptied and scrubbed out), she suggested that we write daily notes to each other, tucking them in with the food. Until I was in second grade, she said I need only draw pictures for her pail. But after that, she expected me to pen something original or copy an extract from a good source.

When I turned eight, Serena began reading me Shakespeare's sonnets, her slender fingers turning each page as if it were gossamer. Coming to the last line of a sonnet, she'd ask, "Did you understand?" Once in a while I ventured a guess, but usually I was uncertain, so we discussed them.

Of the many sonnets, I had favorites, of course. After I'd forgotten to make my bed and tidy my room and was feeling contrite, I wrote to Serena,

> When in disgrace with fortune and men's eyes,
> I all alone beweep my outcast state,
> And trouble deaf heaven with my bootless cries . . .

How grand and important I felt knowing that "bootless" didn't mean going without boots but, rather, "hopeless" or "unavailing."

At dinner, Serena told me that when she read the folded note at lunch, she laughed out loud. The teacher across the hall poked her head in to ask what was so funny. Oh joy, to make Serena laugh! It wasn't very hard, but her laughter always made me feel I'd earned a gold star.

On my tenth birthday, when I was allowed to wear my party dress to school, Serena folded a special note into my pail. "Shall I compare thee to a summer's day?" it read. "Thou art more lovely and more temperate." How I swanned through geography and penmanship that afternoon.

If you are wondering why I call my mother Serena, and always did, well, it's because she was childlike—"fey," I think the word is. And it is my limited observation that teachers of grammar, locution, and literature are often of this nature. Serena and I were more like intimate friends than mother and daughter. We drank tea, real tea, from my set. We played house, recited verses, and were very silly together, making faces, laughing at the same things—for instance the way Mrs. Bullfinch next door invited every traveling salesman into her parlor to demonstrate his wares and to listen as her plump fingers beat out "Champagne Charlie" on the piano, while her outmoded soprano quavered and wavered the verse like a trinkling little waterfall.

Vibrato notwithstanding, Mrs. Bullfinch piped with gusto, "Champagne Charlie is my name . . . Roguein' and stealin' is my game. I got drunk last night and all the nights before; ain't gonna get drunk no more." This she followed with "Whispering Hope," at which point Serena suggested that the commercial traveler was likely whispering hope that the recital might be nearing an end.

And what of my darling Denton? With his silken moustache and dark Byronic looks (Serena had shown me a picture of the poet; she admired the Romantics), Denton was the handsomest man in Beardsley. He taught me to waltz and two-step. He called me "Ruby, my jewel," and the other girls in Miss Jensen's sixth grade were Nile green with envy. His deep voice made me feel safe and cosseted.

Serena and Denton were, I was later told, too happy and devoted to live. That's the sort of thing people said in those days. Maybe they still do. "Happy and devoted" was a death sentence. And, sure enough, the end came for them in a hired sleigh one winter night.

When my mother left me with my great-aunt Bertha that fateful evening—Mrs. Bullfinch wasn't available—the old woman asked with characteristic scorn, "Why in heaven's name would you hire a sleigh to ride into the country just because the snowfall is 'too beautiful'?" Aunt Bertha was as cold-blooded as the ordinary garden skink. But I understand the "why," even if she didn't. Other than a man kissing you on your ruby birthmark and pressing his body against you, a beautiful snowfall is the closest thing to magic that can be found.

At Aunt's, I spent the evening reading *Little Women* and wandering to the front window to look for Serena and Denton. Pulling aside the lace curtain, I saw that indeed the snowfall was too beautiful. And there was so much of it. Drifts and drifts.

"Don't muss the curtains," Aunt Bertha admonished. "They were starched in October and I don't want to do it again until May." Not that Aunt had starched them herself; Beatrice, her hired girl, did that sort of thing.

No matter how many times I crossed to the window, I did not see my parents coming up the walk. In the dining room adjoining the parlor, Aunt sat at the table reading the Bible and sighing, impatient for bed but unable to retire until I was fetched. Her hands lying on either side of the splayed gold-edged pages were knotted, the veins like blue worms crawling beneath the skin.

At some point she fell asleep, sitting straight as a gatepost. On the brown velour sofa, I too dozed but woke with a start when Aunt cried, "Good heavens! It's past midnight and they're not back." She hurried to the window, slapping the curtains aside.

"Frivolous, inconsiderate people! They're out there dead somewhere."


The next morning—in that year of 1910—a uniformed constable came to tell us that a farmer had found Serena and Denton frozen, their lame horse nearly dead. Later in the day, Aunt sat me down on the brown sofa and told me that I would stay with her until other arrangements could be made. She entertained no desire to accommodate a penniless twelve-year-old orphan frivolous by birth.

From our rented house on Chestnut Street, I was allowed to retrieve a tintype wedding portrait of my parents, the tea set, some of Serena's books, and a small painting by Clarice Manetti, a teacher of art at the college: the bank of a stream where a cowherd lay in dappled sunlight, in the background cows coming down to drink. Something about the cowherd had pleased Serena, and it pleased me. The sunlight, eternal in the cowherd's world, played kindly with his pale hair and winsome features. I thought I would marry him when I grew up. When I told Serena this, she said, "I shouldn't wonder. He looks like a boy who reads Keats."

Beyond these few treasures, all else would be sold to pay for Serena and Denton's burials.

"Not that books and sheet music and a few sticks of furniture will pay for much," Aunt disparaged.


A weeping Mrs. Bullfinch sang "Whispering Hope." In addition to Aunt and me, the funeral in the Congregational church was attended by both my parents' colleagues. Aunt admonished me beforehand not to make a fool of myself by carrying on, but everyone's kindness nearly undid me in the vestibule after the service.

"Your mother was such fun," Miss Greene told me. "She always had a little joke or a pretty line of poetry to share."

"And her laugh was beautiful," Miss Harold added. "Like music. It made you happy just to hear it."

"She was kind to everyone. Even had a good word for . . ."

Here, Mr. Heppworth, the typing and bookkeeping teacher, leaned close. "For Principal Evans." He nodded, certain that I understood.

Doctor Barnes, dean of the normal school, patted my head and assured me that one day in the faculty smoker my father had described me as "an enchanting child." Smelling strongly of cigars, the man hooked his thumbs into his vest pockets and smiled smugly. Patting me once more, he moved on to mingle, never looking back.

But young (a master's degree at twenty-two!) Barrett Cromwell, Denton's fellow mathematics and physics professor and a dear companion of both my parents, took my mittened hands in his and told me, "Try to be strong, little Ruby. Your loss is great." Unlike my aunt, he said, "If you wish to weep, that is your right. It isn't a weakness. And if ever you need me, you can reach me at the college. Drop me a line from time to time." Tears gathered in his eyes as he studied me, as if to memorize my face. "You remind me so much of your mother," he said, then bent and kissed the top of my head.


Following the funeral, Aunt told me that my parents' coffins would be stacked in the little brick building by the cemetery gate, awaiting the spring thaw. The next day, she explained that she would turn to Reverend Bass, the Congregational minister, about my future.

Why Aunt Bertha disliked me and my mother before me, I did not understand. I could not see that we had done her any unkindness. On the contrary, Serena had tried her best to be a thoughtful niece. The night of the fatal sleigh ride, she'd brought Aunt a tin of holiday cookies in consideration for watching me. Aunt's dislike was a mystery.

At any rate, when all was said and done, a place was found

for me with "God-fearing people" in Salisbury, a town in north-central Iowa, near the Minnesota border. I knew nothing of Iowa nor of Minnesota except where they were on a map in my geography book.

In lieu of Aunt, Reverend Bass saw me off at the station. The train carried me across the Mississippi River, west and north to Salisbury. For the first few hours, I took Professor Cromwell's advice and shed a million tears. I wept for the only place I'd ever known, the only house I'd ever lived in, the only parents I would ever have, darling Serena and Denton. One day, when I had money, I would come back to Beardsley and visit them. If they were buried in paupers' graves, I would buy them each a beautiful tombstone. On Serena's, the mason would carve, "O, she doth teach the torches to burn bright" from *Romeo and Juliet*, and on Denton's, "A woman would run through fire and water for such a kind heart" from *The Merry Wives of Windsor*.

From the train window as we departed, I could see the cemetery in the distance, even the brick house where Serena and Denton lay waiting for spring.

## CHAPTER TWO

A n elderly, God-fearing couple met me at the Salisbury depot and introduced themselves as Herr and Frau Oster, German Lutherans. I had been intended for Congregationalists, but that family had suffered a tragedy and plans were altered. Through the local newspaper editor, this silent couple fell heir to me. They seemed, if not sanguine, at least resigned. Herr Oster helped me into the buggy. Someone from the depot would deliver my small trunk later.

I had never seen, nor could I easily imagine, a mud fence, though the expression "homely as a mud fence" was common. Herr and Frau Oster, however, must surely be archetypical of mud fences if homeliness was the criteria and, by homeliness, I mean a lack of beauty or notable features. The Osters had faces their own mothers could not pick out in a crowd.

Describing an exceedingly plain face is difficult. Nothing grabs the attention. In fairness, however, Frau Oster did possess a colorless mole of compelling proportions on the tip of her chin. But, otherwise, her face was a bowl of vanilla pudding.

Likewise, Herr Oster owned a single identifying mark, one

ear that stood out from his head a good deal more than the other, like the handle of a pitcher. And as he was deaf in the opposite ear, he often tilted his head, lending a further impression of a pitcher being emptied.

The house we approached was as plain as the Osters themselves. No trim or furbelow was lavished on it. Plain white clapboard, without shutter or scalloped shingle or bit of latticework anywhere evident. Nor had the builder squandered a precious penny for etched or stained glass. And no syllable was frittered on the ride, nor when next we alit in a rutted drive. Without a word, Frau Oster led the way to the front porch. Next to "homely," "laconic" is the word most apt for the Osters. And inside, Frau Oster indicated with a nod that I was meant to climb the stairs to the second floor. I followed her to a small bedroom of conspicuous simplicity: an iron bed with white feather tick, a small table, a chifforobe, and a picture of the child Jesus at prayer. The walls of the room were covered with a white-on-white wallpaper that resembled feathers in a blizzard, the ceiling was white beadboard.

When my trunk arrived, I placed the precious tintype of my parents on the table and two or three of Serena's books on the lower shelf. The rest I stacked in the bottom of the chifforobe. The painting of the cowherd I stood atop the same bureau. Tomorrow, I would find a place for the china tea set, wrapped piece by piece in my clothes.

As I was to learn, the feather tick was a mixed blessing. While it *was* warm, it was filled not with eiderdown but, rather, chicken feathers from the Osters' own fowl. Chicken feathers, even small ones, have sharpish quills that pierce the tick and needle you when you're trying to fall asleep.

Though plain and laconic, the Osters were not unkind. I had thought that I might be their hired girl, but they registered me in the public school. For that I will always remember them fondly.

This is not to say that chores weren't expected. In the backyard a chicken coop housed a substantial number of tenants, and it was my duty to feed them and collect their eggs. The hens were possessive, the rooster combative. The first morning, the biddies complained in full voice as I tried to gather the eggs. Seeing that I was new, they took advantage, two of the hens pecking my hand and drawing blood, the rooster chasing me around the backyard in the snow. However, by the end of the week, I had taken their measure, and began to enjoy stealing from them. At this, Frau Oster said *"Gut."*

As winter gave way to mud and crocuses, Frau Oster assigned me two additional chores. In the morning—when I'd gathered eggs and fed the chickens—I was to scrub the front and back stoops; and after school, I worked in the garden. The Osters were prodigious gardeners. While the front yard was given over to grass and flowers, the backyard was taken up with poultry and vegetables. Frau Oster spent four or five hours a day planting, fertilizing, watering, and weeding. If we were without rain for a week, we drew water from the cistern beside the back door. After school, I changed into an unknown boy's overalls and fell to my hands and knees beside Frau Oster, kneeling in horticultural prayer. Home in the evening from his job at the county court house, Herr Oster joined us, working until the light was gone, stopping only to eat supper.

One day in April, Herr Oster carried home from the post office a letter whose round postmark read "Beardsley, Illinois." As he handed it to me, my heart jumped into my throat. Who on earth could be writing me from Beardsley? It wouldn't be Aunt. Turning the envelope over, I read, "Barrett Cromwell, 326 Augustus Street." Denton's colleague! Eyes dimmed, I climbed up the stairs to my room. Though it was time to lay out supper, this letter wouldn't wait.

*Dear Ruby,*

*Whenever I walk past the house where you lived with Denton and Serena, I think of you and wonder how you are faring. Following a rather unpleasant exchange, your great-aunt Bertha at length parted with your address, and I can only trust that you are still in Salisbury. If you should leave there, please keep me apprised of your whereabouts.*

*I am completing my doctorate and now head the Science and Mathematics Department at the normal school. With the promotion comes a welcome rise in income. I am more than happy to share that rise with you, little Ruby, if you have need of it. Now or later. Do not hesitate.*

*My life is quiet. When the teaching day is ended, I spend a good many hours working on a quixotic project having to do with automobile engines, of all things! I will not bore you with details. It is nothing that could possibly interest a delightful thirteen-year-old girl. You are thirteen now, correct?*

*I miss Serena and Denton. I can only imagine your grief. Your parents were great fun and so kind. I hope that the world is treating you as they treated me.*

*I hold you in my thoughts.*

*Your servant,*
*Barrett Cromwell*

I lay back on the bed and wept, soaking the cotton fabric beneath my head. After fifteen or twenty minutes, Frau Oster ventured a quiet knock at the door and poked her head in.

"Bad news, yes?" She came to the bed looking concerned and proffering me a clean handkerchief.

I shook my head and handed her the letter, unsure if she

could read or understand it. She spent minutes poring over it, her large brow furrowed, one hand twisting a strand of loose hair as she concentrated. I was moved by her desire to grasp the contents. At last she nodded. "It remind you of Mama and Papa, yes?"

I nodded. "But also, it's just so kind. Sometimes kindness can make you cry. You see?"

"*Ach, ja.* I see." She bent and patted my cheek. "You come when you ready," she said, and left.

Before going downstairs, I wept a little more because Frau Oster too was kind. What a weeping fool I was becoming.


Before bed that night, I penned a note back to Professor Cromwell.

"The kindness of your letter overwhelms me," I wrote. "Wherever Serena and Denton are—and I believe they are in a warm and sunny place, living in a big airy house with a cupola— they would send their greetings and affection. And their gratitude for your generosity.

"I thank you for your offer to share the raise that came with your wonderful doctorate, but there is no necessity. The Osters with whom I am living provide everything I need.

"When I think of Serena and Denton, and that is hourly, I imagine all of us in that big house, standing around a piano which Mrs. Bullfinch is playing. The windows are thrown open and we are all singing 'Bill Bailey, Won't You Please Come Home' and 'In the Good Old Summer Time.'

"Serena has made iced tea, and you have brought eclairs from the bakery. We eat a bit and sing a song and Denton tells a joke, something about President Roosevelt and his horse.

"When I imagine us around the piano, time slips away. I am able to do this many times a day, making myself happy again and again."

. . .

The Osters and I attended two church services on Sundays, both in German. With a rare and welcome resort to words, Frau Oster told me that I could bring along something appropriate to read. I chose Walt Whitman, whose aptness she might have questioned had she known, but on a warm June Sunday, surely even the Lutheran minister could entertain no quibble with "Me Imperturbe."

"O to be self-balanced for contingencies," I read, "to confront night, storms, hunger, ridicule, accidents, rebuffs, as the trees and animals do." I did not always understand Whitman, but these words were clear and they appealed. *I* would like to be ready for all contingencies. At the same time, I couldn't help wondering if I were made of such stern stuff. Or was I like the peonies whose unearthly beauty and soft, fragrant petals had been pounded, tattered, and scattered by a storm the previous week? Then I had run into the front yard, gathering petals in my fists and weeping.

"*Nein, nein,*" Frau Oster murmured, patting my shoulder and plucking a red zinnia for me.

When school let out for the summer, Frau Oster added house chores to my duties. Now, I scrubbed the painted floors upstairs, cleaned the oak ones downstairs, then waxed and polished all. In Beardsley, I'd only had to keep my room clean, set the table, wash dishes, and help with sweeping and dusting occasionally. Still, the Osters fed and clothed me and did not mistreat me. And though they were mostly silent, I learned that this silence had grown out of the loss of a child several years before, a boy named Rudolph. After this, I felt a painful tenderness toward them. So plain, so silent, so lonely, for I was not *their* child. If I'd been a tot when I came, perhaps they could have taken me for a surrogate. But I could not have replaced Rudolph any more than the Osters could replace Serena and Denton. People are not interchangeable.

In early summer of my third year with the Osters, news arrived from across the ocean that they had been named heirs to a small estate in Bavaria. We had just come in from the garden and were washing up when someone knocked at the front door. A message had come to town on the telegraph wire. The Osters were dumbfounded by the news of their good fortune. Well, not *dumbfounded*, for they cried *"Gott im himmel"* over and over, dancing around the kitchen, laughing and weeping and hugging each other. At length Frau Oster stopped dancing and, taking her husband's cheeks in her rough hands, asked, "What of Rudolph?"

Then they sat down at the table, Herr Oster across from his wife, massaging his fists with old grief as he looked to her. She shook her head in bewildered dismay, her broad, plain face a painting of sorrow.

Moments before, they had been so happy.

All that evening they spoke in low voices, taking turns to pace. I finally climbed the stairs, put on my nightgown, and lay on the bed, gazing out at the night sky. Those same stars had earlier shone over Bavaria. Now where would I be sent, I wondered.

By morning, the Osters had decided that they would sell the house, buy passage to Europe, and have Rudolph's casket disinterred and shipped across the ocean, if not on *their* ship, then on another. They asked me if I wanted to come with them to Bavaria, but I told them, after some thought, that I would not be happy an ocean away from Serena and Denton.

The newspaper editor was consulted, and word went out that a strong, healthy fifteen-year-old girl with good references was looking for a place. Long before the Osters left on an early October sailing, I was on my way to a farm outside a town called Harvester in southern Minnesota to work for a family named Schoonover.

The depot lay at the northernmost edge of Salisbury, and as we stood on the dusty platform that afternoon, a hot September wind blew off the prairie, pressing our skirts tight against our legs. Again and again, a tearful Frau Oster took me into her arms and called me a "fery *gut* girl." Perhaps they had come to think of me not as a replacement for Rudolph, of course, but as another of their children.

Frau Oster had packed a lunch for me in a small pasteboard box. With each embrace, we crushed it between us. When the train arrived, my trunk was loaded onto the baggage car, and a now tearful Herr Oster shyly pressed two dollars into my hand. I was helped up the iron steps by the conductor, and found a seat by a window looking out at the Osters and Salisbury.

As the train drew away, the three of us waved until we could see each other no longer.

# CHAPTER THREE

A round five o'clock, the train pulled into a station so like the one in Salisbury, I would have thought we'd traveled in a circle had "Harvester" not been printed on the side of the gray building.

On the platform, a lone woman stood waiting. The brim of her straw hat fluttered in the prairie wind. Drawing the sleeve of her dress across her brow, she wiped away perspiration. Advancing, she greeted me. She was Emma Schoonover, she said, and I was to call her Emma. She had not expected a *pretty* girl, she went on. *Was I pretty?*

From the tone of Emma Schoonover's words, *pretty* was something she had not bargained for nor desired. She quickly bethought herself, however, and cast me a flickering smile. She was brusque without being cold. I believe "harried" is the word I want. September was, after all, an extremely busy time on a farm. This I knew from living in two farm towns before coming here.

As we waited for my small trunk to be lowered from the train and carried by the depot clerk to the woman's buggy, I glanced sidelong, trying not to gawk. Emma was perhaps forty and comely without being beautiful, or so I thought at the time. Possibly farm life had robbed her of earlier beauty.

"Up since four a.m." she explained, as if I'd inquired. "Big breakfast for the threshers." Eggs, steak, homemade bread and gravy, pies, egg coffee.

Her spine as straight as a ruler, Emma held the reins loosely but with authority. As we rode out of town, I admired the endless prairie sky, blue as a delphinium.

Emma Schoonover spoke little on the remainder of the drive to the Schoonover farm west of Harvester. She did tell me that Mr. Schoonover was "Henry," and asked if I knew how to milk a cow, which I did not.

"I can gather eggs, though."

Driving along, raising a feather boa of dust behind us, we passed first the Protestant and then the Catholic cemeteries on our right, both beautifully planted with trees and flowering bushes. And so many bodies planted as well! Headstones were thick on the ground.

The earliest days on the farming frontier had been perilous, and they were not long past. Men and women died of exposure, disease, suicide, farm accidents, and half a dozen other causes. The blizzard of '88, I would learn, took hundreds. The loneliness of the wide, mostly empty prairie found a way to claim folks.

Beyond the cemeteries, the buggy turned in at a tree-lined and graveled drive leading to an impressive white clapboard house with a broad front porch, nicely turned columns supporting its slanting roof. The yard lying immediately before was a haphazardly mowed swath of grass sloping down to the road we'd traveled, Cemetery Road.

A big dog of unknown breed and mottled coat—tan, brown, white—came flying down the drive with a great hoo-ha of greeting, barking us all the way to the back gate. "Big lummox," Emma said with fondness as she drew the buggy up. "Name's Teddy, after Roosevelt."

The front door, I'd discover, was rarely used. Even guests and commercial travelers came to the back. The graveled farmyard around us was girded by a cow barn, a horse barn, a pig sty, and a machine shed, all of them painted a rich red. Beyond the machine shed stood corn cribs and silos. A small village of structures. Canny and prosperous, these people were hardworking too.

Parked around the yard were several wagons, their horses let out to pasture till their owners claimed them at the end of the day. "Threshing hands," Emma said. Nearby farmers and their hands came to help with the overwhelming task of threshing the grain; when the crew finished here, they and Henry and his hired men would move on to the next farm in the rotation. If dry weather continued, the grain on all the farms would soon be ready for storage and sale.

"Dennis will carry your trunk in later," Emma told me. "One of our hired men," she explained.

Off to the right of the screened back porch was a big chicken coop. And, to the right of that, a garden, fenced with chicken wire. As Emma and I stepped down, softly clucking chickens greeted us, preoccupied with pecking for seeds and grain in the grass and dirt. They were like old women intent upon their knitting but murmuring to one another. Outside the screeching gate, but not ten yards distant from the back door, stood a watering trough and a windmill clacking with the incessant prairie wind.

Lost in dreams, perhaps, our somnolent buggy horses stood idly nickering as I followed my employer through the gate, across a short brick walk, up three steps, and into the screened porch, which smelled of sour milk. Another thing I was to learn: on a farm, even the most scrupulously clean back porch smells of sour milk. I don't know why, but you get used to it. At the other end of the porch was a screen door leading to the four-hole outhouse.

One hole for Emma, one for Henry, and two for the help, which included me of course. In those days, the outhouse was something you grew up with, its reek one more thing you got used to, along with iridescent-green-winged flies buzzing continually in warm weather.

Raising an arm and pointing, Emma said, "Over there, past the garden, is the storm cellar." It seemed a long way to dash in the event of a tornado. She went on, "We keep last year's apples and carrots and potatoes in there. Also some butter, milk, and ice from the lake."

Inside the house, Emma carried my hat, carpetbag, and gloves to the parlor. When she left to unhitch the horses, I took the opportunity to look around the big kitchen, which was clean and tidy. In two corners, spiral ribbons of flypaper hung from the ceiling, lightly speckled with corpses. These ribbons were not so heavy laden as the ones I'd seen in the Salisbury depot. Emma probably renewed them often during warm months.

Returning to the house, Emma seized a vast apron from hooks behind the kitchen door, thrusting it at me and grabbing another for herself. "Set the table," she said, "while I get the chicken frying." She nodded toward a tall cupboard where dishes were stacked. "There'll be eight places. You and I'll eat after." From shelves beside the woodstove, she pulled a huge and weighty iron spider with both hands, heaving it onto the stove.

Because the Schoonover farm didn't claim a summer kitchen (most in these parts didn't), this one was "hotter than a desperado's pistol," as Mrs. Bullfinch back in Beardsley would have said. Seeing me wipe my brow on my sleeve, Emma told me, "They want hot meat, even in this weather." Shaking her head, she poured liquid lard into the spider. "They won't be in from the field for at least another hour, but we have to be ready. Soon as they wash up out back, they want food."

I began setting plates and utensils on the long pine table,

nervous about what was to come. What kind of men were these? Crude? Loud? Disrespectful? Emma's remark that she hadn't been expecting a pretty girl made me wonder.


The men were dusty with wheat chaff. Though they'd washed their faces and hands and made a pass at brushing off the worst, the dust was in their ears, their hair, and the creases of their clothing, and they were too hungry to care. Hunger subdued their voices until they'd filled their bellies, and it robbed them of interest in a new hired girl.

As they trooped from the kitchen after the final cup of coffee, laughing and chiding one another, they did cast sidelong glances at me as I carried away the remains of their meal. Several nodded. The next evening, when I'd been accepted as *truly* the new hired girl, they would introduce themselves.

Following supper, the men returned to the field where they worked until no light remained. Then the visitors hitched up their horses and headed back to their homeplaces while the Schoonover hired men, Dennis and Jake, sat on the back steps smoking in the dark. Meanwhile, Emma and I had washed up, swept the kitchen and tidied. Now we dished out supper for ourselves, and sat down at the table. Eventually, Henry would join us, sipping a tot of liquor and reading something "picked up at Kolchak's livery."

With the clatter of dinner ended, silence settled over the farm: only the singing of crickets beyond the open window, the occasional squawk from an awakened hen, and the soughing of cottonwoods in the grove gave evidence that the world hadn't wandered off, leaving the three of us in a pale ochre circle of lamplight.

Buttering an ear of corn, Emma told her husband, "This is the new girl, Henry. Her name's Ruby."

He lowered his handbill, glanced at me, and nodded.

"How-do." Another time, he would have conversation, a time when he wasn't weighted to the chair with exhaustion.

"Well, what did you think?" Emma asked me, pouring herself a glass of buttermilk.

I knew what she meant. "They seemed nice enough," I remarked of the men who'd sat at the table. "They weren't fresh."

We exchanged few words after that, both of us worn out.


Later, carrying a kerosene lamp, Emma showed me to my small room under the eaves on the third floor, the climb speaking to her endurance after a hard day. My room was separated from another bedroom by a long storage closet. Nodding at the door down the hallway, she said, "Men sleep there. If they bother, you let me know." Setting her lamp on a bureau, she opened the dormer window overlooking the front yard and Cemetery Road. "I expect they won't. They're pretty good men. But you never know, do you, what men'll get up to?" She lit the lamp on the bedside table. "Better get to sleep real quick. Morning comes early."

Someone had filled a pitcher beside the basin on the bureau, so I undressed and sponged off before pulling on the batiste gown Frau Oster had given me. Before anything else, though, I knelt and opened the trunk, which stood beneath a row of hooks high on the wall. With delicacy, I lifted out the china tea set, a piece at a time. Near the window facing the road sat a wooden box, maybe meant as a seat, but I laid out the tea set on it, just *so*, as I always did. Now the room held some exhalation of Serena.

The painting I hung by its wire from one of the hooks. Though the cowherd lay with his arms folded behind his head, seeming to study the moving water of the stream, sometimes I felt that from the corner of his eye he studied me as well.

I hung my dress and undergarments on the hooks, as there

was no wardrobe, then slipped a book from my carpetbag. Before settling down to read, I crouched by the window, listening to the night, the frogs and crickets, the trees and windmill. The clacking of the windmill was nearly incessant. It would grow so familiar that I would stop hearing it.

I lay down with *Wuthering Heights*, part of my legacy from Serena's library. The rest of the books were still in the trunk. Later, I would pile a few on the lower shelf of the bedside table as I had done at the Osters'. *The Osters*. They'd soon be gone from Salisbury and from my life, nearly as vanished as Serena and Denton.

But now I opened the book to the page where I'd left the story. Nursed by the Lintons after their dog had attacked her, Cathy was home again. Heathcliff, mistreated and banished by Earnshaw at Christmas, was angrier than he'd ever been, and swearing vengeance. Nothing Cathy said could soothe him. They were both orphans and had always clung to each other, but Cathy was of the family, whereas Heathcliff was a mongrel, a child of unknown origin, despised by the Earnshaws.

Some in this world might label me a mongrel, but I had known my parents, dear Denton and Serena, and the book in my hands was proof of it.


For the remainder of that week, every minute was crammed with chores, and it remains a whirling blur. Besides gathering eggs, weeding in the garden, and helping Emma with the three main meals, I carried sandwiches, cool water, and slices of melon down to the threshing field mid-morning and mid-afternoon.

During the all-too-brief window for threshing, the men worked at least fourteen-hour days, six days a week, and sometimes Sunday after church as well if the weather promised fair. One never knew when rain might gather in black, pendulous

clouds above South Dakota and come sweeping over the lip of
the prairie. Nowhere else and never since have I seen men or
women work as they did during those late summer days.

"Next week, when the extra help is gone, I'll teach you to
milk a cow," Emma told me as the threshing began to wind down.

Out of the blur, people's names began attaching themselves to faces. The hired man from the farm directly across
Cemetery Road was Moses Good, the farmer Roland Allen, his
wife Dora. Though the wives of other farmers came with potato
salads and pies during the threshing, we did not see Dora, who
had a month-old baby girl at home. Roland was notable among
the men for his beauty. Emma said that six years ago, when he
was seventeen and had taken over the farm from a homestead-
ing uncle, Roland had been the object of sport among the men
on account of his looks.

"They called him Adonis Allen." She paused from dredging
steaks in seasoned flour. "Men don't quite trust a fellow who's that
good looking. They're always waiting for some shoe to drop." A
moment later it seemed to occur to her that a sheltered fifteen-year-
old might not understand, and she turned to look at me.

"I think I know what you mean," I said. "I read a lot." I laid
a glass at each place on the table. "And Serena told me about
Lancelot and Queen Guinevere."

She did not indicate whether she knew of Lancelot and
Queen Guinevere, but inquired, "Serena?"

"My mother."

"You called her by her first name?" Her tone was wondering.

At suppertime, I studied Roland Allen as much as I could
without appearing to. Beneath the chaff dust, there was no
question that he was beautiful, the most beautiful man I'd ever
seen. The summer sun had bleached his blond hair nearly
white, and his brows were white against skin tanned golden,
dark lashes framed eyes the intense blue of bachelor's buttons.

Ringing each iris was a thin black line which only heightened their intensity.

I would not ordinarily stare at a man, and I soon grew self-conscious and embarrassed to be doing just that. At last I drew myself away to fetch the pitcher of buttermilk from the icebox. There is something about extreme beauty that is like a terrible accident—from which, people say, they cannot look away.

Lying in bed, the lamp still burning, I gazed at the picture of Serena and Denton. Well, darlings, here I am. On a farm now. The Schoonovers are good people. Hardworking. Oh my, yes, hardworking. But the work does them proud. They thrive on it, though it wears them down to their essentials. Remember, Serena, you used to say that about teaching. "It's wearing me down to my essentials, but I love it."

Ah, Serena. Where are you now, you and Denton? Lying back on wicker chaises on a wide green lawn beneath spreading trees? Or perhaps you've drifted on a cloud across the world to far Xanadu, where Kubla Khan "a stately pleasure dome" did build? More than two years have passed since you left, but some of your time is spent with me here in this small third-floor room. I know.

# CHAPTER FOUR

D ear Professor Cromwell,
    Threshing is behind us here on the Schoonover farm and today, as promised, Emma taught me how to milk a cow. When one gazes at cows from a little distance, they don't look so very imposing. Gentle creatures, one would say, who like to lie about and chew their cud. But when one is sitting on a small stool with one's head pressed against their enormous sides, the perspective is quite different.

For one thing, their cruel-looking hooves are in close proximity, and their huge heads, even in stanchions, are likely to swivel to the side in order to shoot one an evil eye if one's inexpert milking technique annoys them. Add to this, the unexpected slap across the face from a none-too-hygienic tail or the sudden, electrical quiver pulsing through their skin when they thrust off a blowfly. Well, one's dreamy imaginings regarding bovines soon dissipate. It's a blessing that the Schoonovers keep only eight

*milk cows and a prize bull whose name is Harold for rea-*
*sons I may one day guess.*

*However, having said all this, Professor, I do look for-*
*ward to perfecting my milking technique.*

As the first frost approached, Emma and I stripped the garden of
produce. What we didn't consume in daily meals, we preserved.
I had never canned before. From a cupboard on the screened
porch, we gathered glass jars, dozens and dozens of them, carrying them into the kitchen where we scrubbed them with hot water and soap, then rinsed them and lowered them into two huge
galvanized tubs filled with boiling water. When the jars were
sterilized, we lifted them out with calipers, drained them, and
set them on the table mouths up, waiting to be fed.

We had prepared whatever vegetable we were canning that
day, washing the beans or corn or tomatoes and cutting them into
appropriate-size pieces. Now we stuffed them into jars and filled
the jars with boiling water and sometimes herbs.

The biggest mess was making mincemeat with the meat
grinder, a complicated tool that fastened onto the kitchen table
and had to be washed meticulously afterward, "If you don't want
to poison a whole family at a meal. Nasty stuff, meat can be, if
you're not careful."

Of the canned goods in general, Emma told me, "If you
don't have everything pure as an angel's kiss, they'll go bad.
And sometimes they explode, and you've got an ugly corrup-
tion to clean up."

When I set the table we usually included a pickle of some variety. At the grocer's back in Illinois, dill pickles came in a barrel,
and Serena or Denton bought a scoop at a time and kept them in a
covered dish in the icebox. Here, we pickled small onions, melon
rinds, cucumbers, beets, and crab apples, and they appeared on
the table in the jars in which we'd pickled them.

Large onions, potatoes, carrots, and, eventually, the bigger apples, went into the storm cellar along with squash and pumpkins. With raspberries, strawberries, and ground cherries, we made jam in season. Some apples became apple butter; some, sauce.

By first snowfall, Emma and I each had a cyst on our wrist the size of a large marble, partly from scrubbing and cutting and stuffing, but mostly from screwing the jar lids closed. Tightly, tightly. Of the cysts, which were new to me, Emma said, "Gone by spring, you'll see."

When the jars of vegetables and fruit were ready, we carried most of them down to shelves lining the cobwebby, windowless space beneath the house, accessible from a door in the kitchen beside the icebox. I often brought up jars from this fruit cellar but never grew accustomed to the dark eeriness of the place.

One day, Emma said, "We'll load some of the canning in the wagon and haul it across the road to the Allens'. Their baby died."

"She died? Why?"

Lifting her shoulders in both bewilderment and resignation, Emma sighed. "Who knows? Took a cold, maybe. Babies die. Some come into the world strong. Some don't." She turned to the sink, pumped water into a glass and drank it. "I lost three. All of 'em boys."

So we packed bushel baskets with fruits, vegetables, jams, and sauces, plus chickens, ducks, and venison, using old towels to cushion the jars. Afterward, we harnessed up one of the horses to the wagon and carried our bounty down the long drive and across the road.

Roland answered the back door, helping us carry the baskets into the house and empty them onto the old kitchen table. In the sunlight, our jars of many colors shone like giant jewels.

Roland insisted that we sit while he made coffee. Emma had come prepared and drew from her huge apron pockets ginger cookies wrapped in rough cloth napkins, cookies she and I had baked that morning.

While the coffee brewed in a chipped gray and white enamel pot, Roland left us to call up the stairs to Dora. Waiting a bit, he called again. Receiving no answer, he returned to the kitchen, shaking his head. "She's a heavy sleeper."

"Don't wake her," Emma said. "We won't be long."

Even in overalls and an old flannel shirt gray with wear at the collar and cuffs, Roland and his intense blue eyes were a sight to inspire an artist. Contemplating him, I felt those eyes were full of questions and unanswered needs.

"So how is Dora getting on?" Emma asked.

Roland shrugged. "All right, I guess. She doesn't come down much. I expect you could figure that, what with the state of the kitchen." He gave the littered counter and greasy stove an unhappy glance, then stirred cream into his coffee and tossed the spoon down with impatience.

"It's hard," Emma said. "It takes time. More time for some than others. Dora's delicate. Always was."

Not quite old enough to understand nor quite familiar enough with these people, I couldn't be sure what Emma meant. Perhaps nothing. But tonight in bed, I would think about Roland and this little scene. Between Emma and Roland there existed a special bond, almost parental.

As we were leaving, he thanked us for the food and pressed my hand. "You're good women," he said. "Maybe someday I can return your kindness." Descending the steps, I put my hand to my cheek and found unexpected heat in the palm where Roland had touched it.

Driving the wagon back across the road, Emma said, "He married a town girl. Pretty but not used to farm work, nor to losing babies, if a person's *ever* used to that. Don't know where it'll end."

In my room that night, I took down the painting of the cowherd and told the blond lad that his name was now Roland.

. . .

With harvest behind us, the men went to work on the machinery—the plow, the harrow, the spreader—sharpening, repairing, painting, oiling, and otherwise getting everything in order for spring. Horse gear was cared for, oiled or varnished. The buggy and wagon the same. Before really cold weather came, the three men worked on the buildings where previous seasons of harsh weather had taken a toll.

I've hardly scratched the surface of the tasks Henry and "the boys" dealt with, side by side. The appellation amused me. Shy Dennis, at eighteen, might qualify as a "boy," but I was pretty sure that Jake was over fifty, his face as weathered, gray, and seamed as an untreated fence post. In many ways, they were like father and son.

However, Emma told me, "Dennis's pa, Mr. Cansler, owns the newspaper over in St. Bridget."

"What's Dennis doing on the farm?"

"Growing up. Been with us two years. Mr. Cansler told Henry Dennis needed 'seasoning' and 'grit.' Come next fall and he'll head off to college. He's a good boy." She handed a spool of black thread and a packet of needles to the clerk in Lundeen's Dry Goods. "I think old man Cansler is a tough nut. Jake's been good for Dennis."

Emma and I had driven the buggy to town, as we always did on Saturdays; Dennis, Jake, and Henry took the wagon. Their tasks and destinations were different than ours. And, after a stop at Reagan's Saloon and Billiards at the end of the day, they would be late returning to the farm.

I can't speak for Emma, but I was always fluttery in my chest and half dizzy in my head on our Saturday trips to town. My breath was short and unreliable as I wandered the aisles of the dry goods store feeling grown-up and a little worldly. After all, I had lived in three different places. Didn't that give me some claim to worldliness? I had rarely shopped with Serena and Denton, however, and never with the Osters, so there were limits to my sophistication.

Standing at the counter in Lundeen's, I gazed around, soaking up the bounty of merchandise, the smells of new cloth and leather, and the feeling of goodwill that Saturday inspired in clerks and customers alike. Lundeen's was everything a dry goods store should be. The varnished floors shone; the counters, tables, and shelves were oak and polished; goods were carefully sorted and neatly piled. Courteous and knowledgeable, the clerks were overseen by the younger Mr. Lundeen, a handsome and well-mannered gentleman of thirty-five or so.

But no words can do full justice to Saturday in town, especially in the warm months, when folks strolled unhurried in the endless evening, promenading up and down Main Street, stopping to trade gossip with someone sitting on a wagon seat or in a buggy. Piano music drifted out the open doors of Reagan's, and you moved along the wooden walk as if in the pages of a novel.

Of course, before the promenading, there were purchases to be made: flour, sugar, thread, dried beans, crackers, maybe fabric or shoes or a new hammer. On one such trip, Emma bought me two cotton dresses, a grass-green with tiny rosebuds and a blue with white daisies. I was filling out, she said, and the sleeves on my old dresses were halfway to my elbows.

Many a farm wife sewed what she or her hired girl needed, but Emma hated the treadle machine. She didn't mind mending, she said, but "making that treadle go with my feet while my hands are tending to the cloth, well, I end up running the needle through my fingers nearly every time."

It was early November now but unseasonably warm. Though we did wear coats (mine would no longer button across my bosom, so Emma had given me an old one of hers), we ambled along

Main Street in the lowering evening like ladies of nobility, pausing in front of the pharmacy to study windows where boxes of Lady Worden's Female Pills and bottles of White Lily Face Wash nudged Dr. Barker's Blood Builder.

As we stood commenting, the door to the pharmacy opened and Roland emerged carrying a large bag and looking startled to see us. Hefting the bag in a kind of greeting, he explained, "For Dora. Something new, called Vin Vitae, the wine of life."

"What's it do?" Emma asked, her head cocked to one side.

Roland removed a bottle, reading from the label. "'A tonic stimulant for the tired, weak, and sick.' Worth a try." Slipping the bottle back into the bag, he glanced from one of us to the other, and Emma nodded. "Well, it's getting dark," he said, thanking us once again for the canned food, then hurrying away.

Gazing after him, Emma shook her head.

Later, my toes would curl in an ecstasy of wonder and happiness as I recalled our meeting outside the pharmacy.

The next afternoon, after church and the midday meal, I told Emma, "I'm going to walk down to the lake. Pretty soon, it'll be too cold."

"There's still a few hunters looking for geese and ducks, so you be careful. Don't get your head blown off. Tomorrow's wash day and I don't fancy doin' it by myself." She laughed.

Sioux Woman Lake was only a mile west on Cemetery Road, but our days were so full, we seldom saw it. In October we did hear guns when the hunters descended, seemingly from everywhere, to bring down the birds as they migrated. Even Henry and the boys went out when they could spare an hour or two. For several days we cooked as many as we could eat, then Emma and I canned the rest.

Around me as I strolled, the autumnal death of leaf and stalk had muted the landscape to pastels in smoky hues. Ahead, the western sky was lowering, the way it sometimes did in winter, plunging till it hugged the earth, hushing all sound. The air smelled of bonfires, from the town and the country, the last of the autumn cleanup before snow covered one's sloth.

Emma and I had cleaned up the yard and garden in October, burning leaves and refuse in a big steel drum. Oh, the heavenly perfume of good clean smoke wafting up to one's bedroom at night when the sky was ebon and the stars icy. Then, one could believe in God. Or something.

I had been reading about pantheism in Serena's book of mythology, and I was nearly won to that way of looking at the world. *Everything* was God or gods. I thought I sensed that feeling in the Whitman as well. I would like to discuss this with someone, but with who? Or was it *whom*?

There, in front of me, through trees now bare, I glimpsed Sioux Woman Lake, the surface gray and only a little ruffled by a nippy breeze that came and went and made me glad I'd worn an old suit jacket of Henry's that hung by the back door. I pulled the collar up and dug my hands into the pockets.

I had hoped to have this corner of the lake to myself, to sit remembering Serena and Denton. Wherever they were, I didn't want to lose them, but someone was sitting on a fallen log, back from the shore, and beneath an oak still hanging onto its brown leaves. Around the lake, this between-seasons time was very quiet, most of the geese and ducks flown south, the fishermen packed up till it was time to auger a hole in the ice and fish through that. When the ice was sufficiently deep, icemen would saw huge chunks of it from one corner of the lake, loading it on a wagon and selling it to those who had fruit cellars dug in their yards and to stores and households for kitchen iceboxes.

The crunch of the petering-out gravel as I neared the lake, caused the seated person to turn. "Ruby." Roland Allen, his voice as smoky as the atmosphere.

"Mr. Allen."

"Roland." He rose, giving himself a little shake, as if he'd been harvesting dreams when I arrived.

"Roland." How wondrous to call the most beautiful man— maybe in the world—by his Christian name.

"Have a seat," he said, indicating the log. "I've been sitting here remembering this time of year back home."

"Was this your favorite season?"

"I think maybe it was."

"Why was that?"

He thought for a moment, then shook his head. "Not sure. The quiet, maybe. Things winding down. What had been done, was done; what hadn't would wait. Sort of like getting ready for bed." He smiled briefly. "Not much of a reason, I guess."

"As good as any."

"What's *your* favorite season?" he asked, as one does out of politeness. He peered out at the lake, still lost in thoughts of home, I surmised. Then, once more, he gave himself another little shake. "What's yours? Your favorite season? No, wait, let me guess. Summer."

"Why do you say that?"

"You're warm and sunny, like summer." He seemed to consider what he'd said. "I mean, well . . . yes, yes, that's what I mean."

"Summer *is* my favorite season. Summer knows what it's doing, what it's about; it's not wishy-washy. It's bright and warm and full of color. I wish it could be summer all year long." I pulled my skirt tight around my legs, protection against the skittery breeze. "I like to lie on the warm grass and look up at the trees and the sky and watch the birds. I like to smell the peonies and roses and mock orange. Sometimes I wish I could *eat* them!" I laughed at myself. "I'm crazy, don't you think?"

"No." He looked sidelong at me. "I think you're . . . wide awake. That's how it sounds. Wide awake. And when I hear you talk, it makes me feel wide awake, like I'm only half awake most of the time."

"Wide awake." I pondered that for a moment. "That's a very nice thing to say."

"It's true."

I saw him tremble. "You're cold," I said. "I'm chattering away, keeping you out in the chill. You should head home."

"No. This is the best I've felt all week, all month."

I hugged myself in a spasm of delight. "Emma said you came from Iowa. What was it like there, where you came from? I lived for a while with some folks in Salisbury. Did you live anywhere near there?"

"You'd like the place I came from. Not near Salisbury, but on the Mississippi, a little burg called Lansing—pretty, on a hillside rising up from the river. There were big boats and barges that rode up and down the river. In warm weather, my dad took me out fishing after work. We fished till dark, my poor mother waiting supper." He smiled. "She's a patient woman."

"So your family didn't farm?"

"My dad's a surveyor. When I came here was the first time I drove a plow horse or milked a cow."

"That must have been a shock."

He laughed. "'Shock' is the right word. But my uncle needed me. He was my dad's only sibling. So it was important. Farming isn't what I'd have chosen to do with my life, but I've learned a thing or two."

"Like what?"

"Soil, good soil, is mystical. Don't laugh. Think about it, Ruby—you put a seed in the ground and, if you get some rain, the next thing you know, something green is pushing up, and I mean *pushing* up, like it can't wait to get to the sun, like it would grow right through the soles of your boots, if you didn't move on. It's magic. Right there, before your eyes."

"Magic." When you stopped to think about it, he was absolutely right. And I did stop to think about it. We were quiet for several minutes.

Then I asked, "What had you *wanted* to be when you grew up?"

"Well, I'd been a pretty good student in high school," he said, glancing at me to see if I thought he was bragging. "My teachers started saying I should go to college, that I might even get a scholarship. I got excited about that. Nobody I knew had gone to college. It sounded, I don't know . . . full of possibilities, like I could make something of myself, something my folks would be proud of. I started thinking about what I'd like to do.

"I thought I might be a teacher. Maybe a history teacher. I liked history in school. Especially ancient history, you know, the Greeks and Egyptians. I wanted to know how they accomplished the things they did.

"Alexander the Great! Think of it, Ruby. He conquered most of the known world. What a man—to have so many follow him into unknown places, places where unimaginable monsters might have been waiting. I wonder why, why did he do it? Curiosity? Power?"

"Maybe he didn't have a choice," I said. "Maybe he just *had* to go there and didn't know why." Without thinking, I blurted, "I wouldn't be at all surprised if he looked like you."

Color rose up his neck and face. My cheeks burned. Quickly, I went on, unsure of pronunciation, but needing to put what I'd said behind us, "Wasn't Alexander tutored by Aristotle?"

Roland looked surprised. "You know a lot."

"Not as much as I'd like."

"That's how I feel. There's so much to know." He rose, heading toward the water, kicking stones. I wondered what he was feeling—regret, longing, bitterness? After a couple of minutes, he turned, shrugging, a chiding gesture that said, *Don't go down that road. That sorrowful old road.*

He smiled, and I wanted to hold him, sharing his sorrow.

. . .

Darling Serena, I whispered into my pillow, I do not know myself. I do not understand these feelings. Do you hear me? Do you recognize the child you left behind? Or am I some new person neither you nor I could have foreseen? And will you help me find my way forward?

The following day, winter was upon us. The previous day's lowering sky should have been a portent.

The large meals continued, and the men's hearts were still wedded to desserts, so pies, cakes, pumpkin bread, or gingerbread were always on the menu. Frequently dessert was sauce, "sass" as Emma called it, with a slice of pound cake. Applesauce was popular, ground cherry sauce not so much. Bread pudding and Indian pudding were great favorites.

During the long winter evenings, the five of us often dealt out cards at the kitchen table. Sometimes it was whist, but more often it was rummy so we could all play. One evening, I ventured to ask Dennis where he'd be going to college after the next year's harvest.

"University of Minnesota. Where my dad went," he said without enthusiasm.

Just the idea of attending a university thrilled me, and I thought of Roland and his loss. I could hardly credit that Dennis was indifferent. Venturing further, I asked, "Where would you *like* to go?"

"Anyplace, as long as it's far away." He reddened. "I mean, you know, back east or out west. I . . . I'd like to see something before I go to work at the paper."

He was still embarrassed, afraid something he'd said might reflect on the Schoonovers and this place, so I asked, "What do you want to study?"

"What I'd really like to study is agronomy." I must have looked mystified. "It's about farming. New ways of doing it, new crops, scientific, you know." He glanced at Henry. "Mr. Schoonover follows all that. He gets these books and pamphlets." He stopped short as if he might be treading where he oughtn't. But Henry was nodding and his eyes were crinkled.

Something about Dennis hadn't caught up with eighteen or nineteen; something unsure was still back there at fourteen. But he was a good-looking boy, tanned and muscled from farm work. There ought to be more strut to him, I thought. More swagger. More eighteen or nineteen in him.

I received another letter from Professor Cromwell. He was still at work on his automobile invention. "I've applied for a patent," he wrote, "and I have other notions I'm playing with. I do enjoy testing and inventing. Am I a bit mad, little Ruby?"

He said that he had stopped by my great-aunt's. Aunt Bertha had apparently warmed to him, as he wrote that she'd begun having the girl make tea on his visits. Well, he was presentable and respectable, not the bohemian-gypsy sort of person she'd said my parents were.

And he described running into my old neighbor Mrs. Bullfinch, she of "Whispering Hope." Mrs. Bullfinch was eager to hear more about my new life, he said. Though I'd written her, she had questions. Did I have a beau? After all, I was fifteen or thereabouts. And, if I were to marry, might she be asked to sing? She'd be only too happy to take the long train ride for such an occasion.

"I think she is coloring her hair," Professor Cromwell wrote further, "though it is unkind to mention it, and it may not be true. Serena once described her as 'quite dear, but fighting age with a Spartan will.'"

In a recent letter, I had tried to draw a true picture of the farm and its people, describing everyone's hard work and their entertainments. "Dear Emma is plainspoken and kind, Henry taciturn and of goodwill." I made a pass at describing Roland and Dora, though I'd never actually seen Dora.

"If you could imagine the statue of David coming to life, Professor Cromwell, you could perhaps imagine Roland Allen. He is sad, it is true, but to tell the truth, I've always thought that the statue of David looked a little sad."

Now he wrote suggesting that I make a point of getting to know Dora. "For how can you know the man if you don't know the wife?"

Of my previous letter, he wrote, "All those books of Serena's that you have been reading have given you a fair gift with the pen. You should be studying in a college. I am sure that the Schoonovers are all that you say, but I worry that your mind isn't being challenged on the farm. It is my dearest wish that one day you'll return to Beardsley."

Finally, he wrote, "I'm enclosing five dollars, hoping that you will buy yourself a treat. An Oklahoma oil company asked me to run a test for them for which they paid handsomely, so do not imagine that you are depriving me of anything by accepting this small gift. I like to think that in a very minor way I am standing in for Serena and Denton."

*Five dollars!*

"Dear Professor Cromwell," I wrote immediately. "I send a wagonload of thanks for your generous gift. With your five dollars I shall have a photograph taken, so that you may see the healthy, hearty girl being nurtured in this rather amazing place.

"I do think that you underestimate all that a farm—even a garden—can teach of seed and maturity; soil and blight; wind and weather; dreams and doubts. For me, this farm is an endless source of wonderment. I am learning so *much* here. You have no idea."

. . .

In my next letter to Mrs. Bullfinch, I wrote, "I don't have a beau, and I haven't been on the lookout for one. I want to be everything Serena wanted me to be: kind and educated. She used to tell me not to marry before I was twenty, so there'd be time for education. Of course, along the path life has taken me, I may not have the opportunity for college, so I read Serena's books and study the dictionary. I confess, I also use Roget's Thesaurus in order to write more intelligently. As you might imagine, I don't want to sound ignorant when I write to Professor Cromwell. He is so brilliant and kind.

"In any case, there aren't many opportunities or candidates for beaux around here. Dennis, the younger of the two hired men, is leaving for college next fall, and the other, Jake, must be fifty if he's a day. Moses, the hired man across the road, is even older."

I wrote of Serena and Denton and when I did, I had to lay the pen down to dab my eyes. Time hadn't yet softened the edges of grief. Even so, I wanted to discuss them with someone who, like the professor, had known them and would join me in keeping them alive.

"Remember how Serena and I made May baskets and left one by your door? When you heard us knock, you came running out and gave us each a hug. We left one at Aunt's, but she didn't come running.

"I am reading Elinor Glyn's *Halcyone*, a book Henry found at the Water and Power Company when he was in town. There's a reading shelf where people leave books they no longer want. Unlike Beardsley, Harvester doesn't yet have a regular lending library."

Toward the end of my letter, I described Roland to Mrs. Bullfinch. "If you had the opportunity to visit an observatory and look through a telescope, and if you found a star that was brighter than the rest, that would be Roland."

"I want to have my picture taken," I told Emma after breakfast one Saturday morning. "Does anyone in Harvester take pictures for money?"

"Mr. Sonnenberg does," she said.

"Do you know how much he charges?" I asked. "I have five dollars. Would that cover it, do you think?"

"Five dollars!" she said, surprised.

"A friend of Serena and Denton's sent it."

"Five dollars'll probably cover it and then some," she said, adding, "wear yer best dress. I'll help with your hair."

Later, as I sat on an extravagant, Egyptian-looking chair— the arms extending into carved Pharaoh's heads—beside a huge brass pot planted with a substantial palm, Mr. Sonnenberg asked, "You don't have a plain, dark dress you could wear?"

"No, sir, this is my best," I explained, smoothing the skirt of my grass-green dress.

And so it was that I sent a small portrait of myself—Minnesota farm girl, a hired one at that, set down a stone's throw from the Nile—to Professor Cromwell and Mrs. Bullfinch, holding one picture back as a present for Emma and Henry and another for the future.

# CHAPTER FIVE

Halcyone, the girl in the book I was reading, was serene, graceful, intellectual, and beautiful. Did I mention enchanting and kind? Those too. She read Greek, French, and Italian. I was growing less fond of her.

But how exotic, to read Greek! Given half a chance, I thought I could be, like Roland, quite fond of Greece. I was delighted by the gods and goddesses, nymphs, and satyrs I found in S.A. Scull's *Greek Mythology Systematized*, another of Serena's library.

However, playing Parcheesi Royal Game of India around the kitchen table was the exotic height to which life soared that late winter of 1915. Jake had sent away for it from a catalog in the outhouse. Whichever catalog came—Montgomery Ward or Sears and Roebuck—it always ended up in the outhouse, its pages used for wiping. If the weather wasn't too hot or too cold, you could while away ten minutes or more poring through them. But if you stayed longer, Emma knocked on the door yelling, "Either pee or get off the pot!"

The Parcheesi board was colorful and, yes, exotic—merely to look at it was a pleasure. The game was played with dice and little wooden pieces that you moved around the board. Imagining that red was my lucky color, I usually chose that piece, but I rarely won. I didn't mind losing. I had the notion that the more I lost at Parcheesi, the more I would win at something else. I expect everyone plays these little win/lose games in their heads, trying to beat fate.

One particular evening, as we were choosing our game pieces, Dennis asked me, "What do you want to do when you grow up?"

I bridled. "When I *grow up*! I'm fifteen and a half years old. Plenty of girls my age are married and having babies. And besides, what makes you think I won't be right here with Emma and Henry 'when I grow up'?"

His ears reddened. "Not sure. Nothing against Emma and Henry." He looked down at the dice in his hand. "You read a lot. You sound like somebody who might be a schoolteacher, that's all."

I was mollified. "My mother was a schoolteacher," I told him. "She was like Halcyone in my book. Cultured and kind and beautiful."

He grinned, a sort of secret grin, as if he thought I might be exaggerating.

"I have a picture of her, of her and Denton, if you don't believe me. I'll get it and you can see for yourself." I climbed the stairs two at a time.

Returning, out of breath, I handed Dennis the tintype and settled myself at the table once more. The rolling of dice had awaited my return.

Dennis took the picture and studied it, nodding. "They're a beautiful couple." He handed it around for the others to see. Dennis was guileless and as transparent as a piece of glass. When he was wrong or mistaken, he admitted it without hesitation or embarrassment.

"You look just like your mama," Emma told me. "Though maybe you got your daddy's chin."

As the fragile brass frame was passed to them, Jake said, "Very nice," and Henry murmured, "Good-looking people."

On the back porch, Teddy growled, a low-down-in-the-throat announcement. We heard him rise from his rug and start for the screen door, his claws scritching on the linoleum.

Crossing the kitchen, Henry opened the door to the porch. "What is it, Teddy?"

The screen door creaked and Roland asked, "All right if I come in, Henry?"

Holding the inside door, Henry motioned the other man into the kitchen. Emma had risen. "Give me your coat." Taking the dogskin coat, she told Roland, "Sit. We're playing Puhcheesi the Royal Game of India. Raw wind out there. I'll get you coffee."

"Don't go to bother."

"No bother. It's on the stove." Hanging the coat on the back of the cellar door, she fetched a cup of coffee and set it on the table. "Dora?"

"Sleeping," he told her.

"This last tonic didn't help?" Emma sat down at her place.

"Didn't seem to."

"Mosta them tonics ain't worth the cost, is my opinion." She nudged Dennis. "Your roll, son. Roland, would you like to play?"

"I think I'll watch."

Dennis rolled the dice and moved the green piece several squares.

Roland had taken the chair next to me, so close I could feel the cold of the March night on him. He warmed his hands on the coffee cup and observed the play. I felt a wrenching empathy for him, for his wife who slept endlessly, for the forlorn dogskin coat, for the shirt that needed mending. For Greece and Egypt.

After the Parcheesi game ended, Emma said, "I'll get the cards. We'll all play rummy."

When six of us played, we used two decks. Emma shuffled each deck separately, then mashed the two together. Jake cut the cards and Emma dealt them out.

As Roland reached for his cards, his knee brushed the side of mine. Despite the interjacency of his cold overalls and long underwear, and of my cotton skirt, petticoat, and wool stockings, a live spark penetrated my leg and flashed upward. I twitched, then glanced around the table to see if anyone had noticed. They were all studying their cards. I gathered mine and rested my hands on the table to steady them. What had just happened? The hot, liquid feeling in my groin was not unpleasant, but my hands were unreliable, weightless and jerky, and my face burned. I wished that I could join Teddy on the back porch.

"Ruby, it's your turn to draw a card," Emma said.

An impulse in my belly made me want to touch Roland—and not merely touch him, but grab him tightly, even cause him pain. Instead I drew a card. I was in no condition to tell if the five of spades fit with the rest of my cards, so I tossed it on the discard pile. Dennis snatched it up.

I didn't win a single hand. "Well, Ruby," Emma said, "unlucky at cards, lucky in love, isn't that what they say?"

I helped Roland into his heavy coat as he prepared to leave. Jake had gone out to check on the horses, and Dennis had climbed the 'the big wooden hill,' as we called the stairs to the third floor. Emma was slicing roast beef and assembling sandwiches for Roland and Dora. As she was wrapping them, Roland pinned me with his gaze, then grasped my hand, holding it briefly to his chapped lips. I smiled inanely.

When he had left, I washed up the few dishes while Emma and Henry sat at the table, Henry sipping a tot of whiskey, Emma another cup of coffee pale with heavy cream and three teaspoons of sugar. Hanging my apron on the same hook that had held Roland's coat, I shuddered once more, then turned, shoveling together the cards scattered on the table and putting them to bed in the cabinet in the parlor.

As I reentered the kitchen, Emma and Henry were discussing Roland and Dora, Emma saying, "I worry she'll end up in St. Peter. He's losing patience, you can tell. And who'd blame him? He's tried. She don't want to get out of bed."

Dennis had told me about St. Peter, the state hospital for the insane—a woman he knew in St. Bridget had been sent there on account of her anger. I was skeptical, but he said it was true, he knew it for a fact: a man could have his wife put away if she was an angry person. I couldn't help thinking of the women who might have good reasons to be angry. Loath to believe such an injustice could be true, I questioned Henry but he, too, had heard of it. Could a man have his wife committed if she slept all the time?

Regarding Dora, Henry was more sanguine. "Her folks'd have something to say about any committal."

Carrying the coffee cup to the sink, Emma replied, "I doubt they'd care."

I said good night and went upstairs with the tintype of my parents. After returning it to the bedside table, I read a few more pages from *Halcyone* but could not concentrate. I kissed my hand where Roland had put it to his lips. What was happening to me? I recalled his eyes, that otherworldly blue with the black ring around the irises. They were seductive, mesmerizing, devouring, as if he would swallow me whole.

"Darling Serena," I said under my breath, "beyond my frosted window, I see a sky full of stars. The sky where they hang is too huge for words to fit. And, Serena, something too huge for words is taking hold of me. I am frightened and happy."

# CHAPTER SIX

I n bed the next night, I continued with *Halcyone*, despite finding her more and more improbable. Once I'd begun a novel, I felt compelled to finish it; after all, the author had gone to a good deal of trouble.

In any event, the plot of *Halcyone* was thickening. And the time had come for a reader—this reader—to grow concerned about the heroine, even one of off-putting perfection. It is the business of novelists to worry readers, and Halcyone had thrown herself headlong into a love affair, albeit a chaste one. The girl was innocent and vulnerable. And how much did she know about this John Derringham?

When he didn't fetch her for their planned elopement, I read with suspicion, that John had fallen into a haw-haw (a *haw-haw*? Well, it is England), broken his ankle, injured his head, and found himself too weak to raise an alarm. Meanwhile, rain poured down in torrents. Would he drown or perish of pneumonia before he was discovered?

The majority of novels I had read involving men and women—and that was surely most of them—were cautionary tales. *Ethan Frome, Wuthering Heights,* and *Great Expectations* to name only three. Apparently, there existed great numbers of girls—and boys too—who were foolish enough to blunder into unfortunate or unsavory love affairs.

The hard work of spring planting left little time for cards and board games. When the men were finally done with the day's work, they had only enough energy to down their suppers before heading to bed.

Weeks passed when I had no glimpse of Roland, though I felt his existence across Cemetery Road, as if a taut wire, a telegraph line, connected us. On my end, electricity coursed through me whenever I thought of him. Around Emma I was careful not to act dreamy or preoccupied. But it was difficult. All I wanted was to sprawl on a parlor chair and imagine myself touching Roland.

Hard work was always at hand, however. Laundry alone was the work of a day and a half, more difficult in cold weather when it all had to be done in the kitchen. On the back porch stood two big wooden tubs, each atop a wheeled stand. These we rolled into the kitchen on wash day. The laundry, in two capacious copper tubs on the stove, soaked clean in hot water and lye soap while we stirred with long wooden paddles.

When Emma determined that things were clean, we transferred the hot, wet fabrics into the first tub, filled with cool rinse water, then through the attached wringer and into the second tub to rinse again. Finally, the laundry was fed through the wringer once more, dropping into a basket on the floor.

I cranked the wringer for Emma while she fed clothes, sheets and household linens into it. "I'm an old hand at this," she said. "I don't want you getting your fingers caught in this contraption. It can break 'em."

"After harvest next September, I'm getting one of those new

wash machines I've seen in the catalogs," Emma told me one day, wiping her red hands on her apron. "Still hard work, but not so bad as this."

Even in deepest winter, sheets, overalls, and dresses were hung on lines in the yard, beyond the apple trees. When we brought them in at the end of the day, the men's frozen overalls stood stiff and upright. Emma waltzed around the kitchen holding one like a dance partner and singing, "Casey would waltz with a strawberry blonde . . ."

Moonshine, the Schoonovers' black horse, pulled the wagon that Henry and the boys drove to town that May afternoon, while Emma and I took the buggy with Sunshine. Unlike poorer farmers in the county, the Schoonovers never used their work-horses for buggy trips. Henry didn't have many faults, but he was proud of the handsome Moonshine and Sunshine.

We took both conveyances this Saturday as the men again planned to end up at Reagan's Saloon and Billiards when they'd completed their stops; Emma and I were headed for the grocery store, the pharmacy, and Lundeen's Dry Goods, to secure Emma a new hat. I wanted to stop at the Water and Power Company, too, where the tall shelves waited for me to return *Tess of the d'Urbervilles* and choose something new for the coming week. I had nearly exhausted Serena's collection.

The afternoon was warm and unusually breathless without the constant breeze swaying the cemetery trees and stirring the gravel dust behind us in the road. Emma said, "Feels queer. Wouldn't be surprised if we'll see a storm before night."

Something of that feeling greeted us as we turned onto Main Street. Folks, town and country, were gathered in knots along the wooden sidewalks, heads bent in quiet conversation. Few looked up as we passed.

Alighting in front of Lundeen's, Emma said, "There's a sign on the door. 'Closed.' Whatever for, on Saturday?" She turned and stopped a woman coming toward us. "What's happened?"

The woman dabbed her eyes and shook her head. "That big ship, real big ship . . ." She struggled to recall the name. "Anyways, it went down. Damned Germans," she said and hurried on.

We crossed the street to the pharmacy, where Emma asked the chemist, "What in heaven's name?"

Like the woman in front of Lundeen's, he shook his head. "*Lusitania*. Kaiser sank it." He paused. "The young Lundeens, George and Cora, gone like that." He snapped his fingers unsuccessfully. "This town won't see their like again."

I recognized the genuine emotion behind the cliched words—almost the same words I had heard at Serena and Denton's funeral. I found I was weeping, and I stepped away. I recalled young Mr. Lundeen, handsome and grave, with old eyes and dark hair beginning to gray.

"They never made it off the ship," the chemist continued. Surely this was conjecture? "Cora, you know, was in a wheelchair." He was overcome and had to look out the front window while he swallowed tears.

Emma moved off, giving him time to collect himself and blow his nose. At length she returned to the counter. "I only knew the young ones to say hello," she said, "but his parents, well, they're royalty."

The chemist picked up on this. "Royalty. But plainspoken and kind. I just hope this doesn't kill them. He's not as young as he used to be."

Leaving with two big bottles of tonic and a small bottle of iodine, we turned toward the grocery store, where, again, there was much murmuring and shaking of heads.

We carried our purchases to the buggy, and I returned my

book to the Water and Power Company, grabbing a copy of *Godey's Lady's Book*. I was suddenly in the mood for something lighter.

After we climbed into the buggy, a silent Emma drove us to the south end of Main Street and the Harvester Arms Hotel, a white clapboard building with a broad front porch where, in summer months, a congregation of wicker rockers faced the street.

"I need a cup of tea and a doughnut," Emma explained as we entered.

Until we were seated with our repast before us, she said nothing. Then, with a napkin spread across her lap, she measured out phrases, picking and choosing, news of the Lundeen deaths freighting her words.

"A person doesn't often come across folks like the Lundeens," she said. "In the pharmacy, I said 'royalty.' Maybe that's not the word I want. They were something more and better than royalty." She paused. "Well, of course, the senior Lundeens still are, bless their hearts."

Idly, she broke her doughnut into two pieces and lay the halves back on the plate. "When Henry's folks first came here, Laurence Lundeen—that's the father of the one who's dead now—was a sprout fresh from college and running a young bank he started with family money. From back east somewhere, he was, and newly married, still wet behind the ears and hoping folks wouldn't notice." She shook her head and smiled. "He was so determined not to lose the money his family had lent him. Scared to death, Henry's pa said."

Now that she'd got started, her tongue was easier. "Henry's pa needed a loan to buy acreage beyond the homestead, but he had nothing to put up, you know, to secure it, except the homestead. And he'd used that for a loan over in St. Bridget to buy machinery and animals."

She finally took a bite of doughnut and a sip of tea. "Well, they sat in Lundeen's office for maybe an hour, Lundeen asking Herman all sorts of questions about himself and the world and where he'd come from. Toward the end, he said, 'Herman, tell me about your marriage. What do you say to your wife when you go to bed at night? Nothing intimate, just conversation.'

"Herman was struck dumb by the question, wondering what it had to do with a loan. He thought a minute or two, then he said, 'Well, mostly I say, 'Ain't we lucky, old lady? We got each other and we got this place and we got a good boy, besides.'"

"And then, Herman told us, Lundeen asked him, 'How much money do you figure you need?' And that was that."

I refilled her cup.

"Lundeen ran his bank on intuition. And his intuition was pretty good. Besides the bank, he owns a lumberyard, a dry goods store, and probably half the town. And nobody begrudges him."

She scrubbed up her crumbs with a nub of doughnut, and popped it all into her mouth. "One day when I was in the store, I heard Laurence say that you could never count on anything but your own character. Something could rob you of everything in the blink of an eye. 'Keep your head down and do good,' he said. That was his motto."

She was quiet for a long moment. "Now, 'something' has taken his son."

I had never known Emma to have so many words or such a philosophical side to her. Did she feel as clearly as I did how fragile everything was? The *Lusitania*'s sinking surely reminded me of a beautiful night when a horse went lame and, all at once, everything was gone.

Once more I felt that emptiness of the universe, how—in some sense—we were each of us alone in it, piloting our own little bark, dependent upon our own strength and resources. Maybe not quite adrift. No, we had *received* wealth. Books, for instance.

I owned everything in the books I had read and I could not be robbed of it. No legacy was greater.

And I owned memories. Memories of Serena and Denton: these were surely a golden cargo. And the memory of all kindnesses and kisses. Stowed in the hold.


Henry and Emma were irregular churchgoers. If pressing work kept them from the Methodist church on Sunday, they did not wring their hands but figured that their god, doubtless a farmer himself, understood.

However, the morning after the awful news of the *Lusitania*, everyone from the Schoonover farm attended church. The Lundeens were Methodists, too, and filling a pew in their honor was a sign of respect.

From the pulpit, the minister explained that he had been with the Lundeens only an hour earlier. In his words, they were "heavy with loss" and looking to the needs of their grandson, thirteen-year-old Larry, now an orphan. "Let us pray for Laurence and Juliet and young Larry," he admonished, and we did.


Though some warned against planting a garden before the end of May, for fear that a late frost would kill it, Emma and I had started seedlings in the house and were impatient to see them in the ground, so one day in the third week of that month, when the air was soft and the sun strong, we went at it, digging small holes and carrying pails of water.

When we'd troweled the last hole, slipping in a squash seedling, Emma said, "I've been meaning to visit the Allens' and see what needs doing. Would you mind taking a look?"

Before I could ask, she explained, "You know—are the dirty dishes stacked halfway to the ceiling? Is the kitchen floor a disgrace? When were the sheets last washed? That kind of thing."

"I don't mind," I said. Of course I didn't mind. I might spy Roland. "But what about Dora's folks? Don't they ever help out? What do they do?"

"They run a hardware store in town, mister and missus both. Strict Baptists, dead set against Dora marrying Roland. They had other plans. A lawyer fellow from St. Bridget. But Dora was bound and determined. Now they've turned their backs." Emma scraped the dirt off the trowel she held. "Maybe if the baby had lived . . . Anyways, we gotta look after Roland. Her, too, if she'll let us." She sighed.

In my room, I shed the filthy apron, quickly sponge-bathed, and combed my hair, pulling it back again and tying it with a fresh ribbon. I couldn't move fast enough. I was trembling and my fingers were clumsy.

Emma was in the kitchen when I came down. "Here's some of the cake we baked," she said, setting a plate on the table for the Allens. "Now, you eat before you leave," she said, "in case there's nothing in that house." She handed me a plate with a chicken leg, a mound of sauerkraut, and a slice of cake.


I ran down the long drive, careful not to spill the Allens' cake. Across the road, all was quiet but for the clucking of hens and the lowing of cattle in the pasture.

At the back stoop, I opened the screen door and called, "Anybody home?" No answer. Stepping into the porch and then the kitchen, I called again, "Anybody home?"

Setting the cake on the table, I glanced around. The kitchen was a fright, dirty dishes everywhere, flies buzzing around them. The floor hadn't been scrubbed since God was a boy. The stairs were off the parlor. I called up, but received no answer. Was Dora awake and refusing to respond? How could anyone sleep this much or want to? How could anyone look at that kitchen and not want to grab a broom and rag?

Rolling up my sleeves, I tossed kindling into the stove, where a bit of flame still flickered. I set a kettle of water from the kitchen pump on the stove, then grabbed a couple of chunks of wood from the bin and shoved them in.

The sink was repulsive. Lifting out the dirty dishes, I grabbed a questionable-looking rag and began to scour the soapstone with baking soda. When the water in the kettle had heated, I poured some into a basin and started on the dishes, no simple task since food had congealed on them.

Half an hour later, when the last of the dishes were washed and dried with clean flour-sack towels from a drawer, I tossed the filthy towels beside the back door to carry across the road. Any other dirty linens I threw into the same pile, nearly retching at the look of them. I didn't scrub the kitchen floor—that would wait for another day—but I did sweep, and I wiped off the table and counter.

Was Dora really sleeping or was she listening to me doing this work? I tiptoed up the stairs. At the top, an open doorway beckoned, and I peeked in. A woman lay on a bed, back to me, a slow rising and falling of her torso indicating deep sleep. I tiptoed away again and down the stairs.

Why, Dora, why do you sleep interminably, letting your house go to wrack and ruin and ignoring your husband? I sat for several moments at the kitchen table, lost in these thoughts.

The afternoon had gone three, and it was time to start back up the driveway and across Cemetery Road. Gathering up the soiled things I had thrown down by the door, I headed out, but paused when I heard someone moving around in the barn. As I approached the wide barn door, two black cats came scurrying out, one with a rat in its mouth. Startled, I yelped and dropped the bundle. Inside, Roland turned toward me. "Ruby?"

I crossed to where he stood holding a pitchfork. He thrust it aside and held out his arms. I walked into them, and now I held him, as I had only imagined doing.

As if we'd rehearsed for years, in one sweet move we tumbled down on the pile of hay, facing one another. First, I held his face and kissed it everywhere, and then I took a fierce hold of his rear with my hands, and pressed his body against mine. Without removing our clothing, we shifted and writhed and turned every which way, twining and locking our legs until I heard myself whimper and Roland groan, "Jesus." Neither the dust nor the scratchiness of the hay could diminish the delirium of the moment. Then the dust made me sneeze, and we laughed and that was sweet too.

Grabbing up the bundle of laundry from the yard, I ran, singing all the way.

I had noticed that in novels, when something momentous happens, the author often spends the following twenty pages analyzing it. Why did it happen? What did it mean? What were the likely consequences?

I did not want to do that. What I wanted was to lock the moment in a tapestry bag with a shiny brass clasp, a bag to hold tight to my breast or to open at will in the future, removing the contents, not to question them but merely to savor them a thousand times. If the scene in the barn was a one-time occurrence, I would carry it in the tapestry bag all my life.

Returning from the Allens' that afternoon, I found Emma in the kitchen.

"So how were things?"

*Lovely.*

"The kitchen was worse than you can imagine. Nearly every dish in the house was filthy."

She nodded, and said, "Go back there tomorrow afternoon and look what needs doing in the rest of the house. I'll do up the laundry you brought, but there's bound to be more. Bed linens at least."

As I laid the table with my back to her, Emma couldn't see the Ruby I had become that afternoon.

# CHAPTER SEVEN

T he Allens' house felt silent and empty. Yesterday I'd
made a racket banging pots and pans, and the noise had
filled the place. Today, my chores, like dusting, were
quiet. The place was ghostly, as if a wraith might meet me around
a corner.

Not that there were *that* many corners—three rooms on the
first floor, probably three on the second, one belonging to old
Moses—but still there was an eerie feeling. I recalled the day by
the lake, when Roland said he felt more alive than he had all that
month.

Emma had sent a bag of rags with me for dusting the furniture, what little there was. I looked for a dry mop, something to
swab up the gopher-size dust creatures lined up along the base-
boards and huddled in the corners. Instead, in a dark pantry off
the kitchen, I located a wet mop with a rag that was gray and
stiff. I sprang open the jaws holding the rag and inserted one of
Emma's clean, soft ones.

Back in the dining room, I dusted the sills of the two windows, then ran the makeshift dry mop over the pine flooring.

From the room above came the sound of a woman's soft step. I
halted, standing stone still. But now, silence. What kept me from
calling out, announcing myself? Why was I sneaking around like
a thief?

I dusted the parlor as I had the dining room, then shook the
mop outside the back door. Roland was not in the farmyard nor
did I see any movement in the barn. Disappointed, I turned back
into the house, reminding myself that I shouldn't expect to see
Roland each time I crossed Cemetery Road.

I opened the parlor door to the stairs. With the dust rag in
hand, I began climbing, cleaning one tread at a time. Reaching
the top, I went back down to collect the dry mop. After mop-
ping the dust creatures in the second-floor hall, I let myself into
what must be Moses's room, a space monastically tidy. Quickly,
I dusted the floor and the sparse furnishings. Beside the narrow
bed lay a stack of Wild West magazines, and on the bureau stood
a chalkware figure of Jesus.

I would leave a note downstairs for Moses, asking about his
laundry. Pulling the door silently to, I moved along to a third
room. Storage? The hinges mewled as I entered. Across the
room, near a double window, an empty cradle stood bathed
in mellow afternoon light. Close by was a low, armless rocker,
a sock doll propped on it. I did not linger, but closed the door
again and descended the stairs.

Reaching the bottom step, I sat down, oppressed. As the chill
of the bare wooden step seeped into me, I shivered. I was jealous
of everything connected with Roland—the cows in his pasture,
the pasture itself, and his dog, Red. I was jealous of Moses. And,
most especially, I was jealous of Dora, who had birthed Roland's
baby.

Additionally, I was filled with guilt for loving Roland. Guilt
and regret are so often linked, but not once in my life would I
think, "If only I hadn't loved Roland."

At last, I pulled myself up, hoping that the source of my jealousy and guilt might yet appear. I swept the kitchen floor and saw to several superfluous chores. Finally, as I was about to leave, I recalled Emma telling me to bring home any further laundry. With the greatest reluctance, I climbed the stairs again and knocked on Dora's bedroom door.

"Dora? It's Ruby from the Schoonovers'. Emma wants me to gather up your laundry." I waited. "Dora? Sheets, pillowcases, maybe clothes?"

She didn't answer, but I could hear her plodding slowly about. I wasn't certain what the silence meant. Was she ignoring me? Would she produce soiled things or was I wasting my time? I sat down on the top step to wait. I would give her the benefit of the doubt. Ten minutes' worth.

I believe she used up the entire ten minutes, during which I grew to dislike her. I had risen to my feet to leave when the bedroom door opened partway and a pale arm reached out and dropped a stuffed pillowcase on the floor. A second pillowcase followed. And then the door was closed.

I wanted to yell, "You know we're doing this out of the goodness of our hearts, you lazy thing!" Out of the goodness of Emma's heart, actually. I didn't think I had any goodness in my heart for Dora Allen. But instead of yelling, I carried the pillowcases across Cemetery Road.

Later I asked Emma if there was a laundry in Harvester. Maybe the Allens could send their dirty things to town. Emma and I already had as much washing as we could handle.

"For a while, a Chinese man and his wife started what they called a 'hand laundry,' but the last I heard, they moved to St. Bridget. Mrs. Krautkammer's sister and niece are taking in laundry, I believe." Emma handed me a stack of plates, meaning I should get on with setting the table. "But," she continued, "Roland couldn't afford hired laundry. And besides, there'd be mean gossip if a farmer's wife wouldn't wash their own clothes."


*Halcyone* having reached a happy ending, I was now well into my *Tess of the d'Urbervilles* and hoping for another such ending, yet wondering what one should make of this Alec fellow. Wasn't there clinging to him an air of indolence and mischief? Beware, Tess, I thought. What an epidemic of cautionary tales! As the dim remains of light faded from my south-facing window, I laid the book aside and lit the kerosene lamp.

Often I asked Serena's advice, and sometimes she seemed to answer me. Or, at any rate, events would turn out in such a way that I felt she had answered me. With Roland, I supposed I would have to leave matters in the lap of the gods, as Serena might say. I could not see my way through to an end. I knew only one thing: the way I felt wouldn't melt away.

Early Saturday afternoon, before we drove to town, Emma and I returned the laundry to the Allens, along with a roasted chicken, potatoes, and gravy. Roland and Moses were in the field, so we set the food on the table and the bundle of washing on the sofa. Emma looked around the kitchen and rolled up her sleeves. "Might as well take care of these dishes."

When we'd washed and dried them, Emma called up the stairs, "This is Emma Schoonover, Dora. I'm headed to town. Anything I can bring back?"

After long moments, a woman's voice, with some irritation, called back, "Two bottles of Mrs. Burnside's Female Tonic." Yet another brand.

"All right." Emma shook her head. To me, she said, "Can you remember that?"

. . .

The following Saturday, when the men returned from Reagan's, Henry was excited, rattling on about the turn the May weather had taken and the sweet scent of the lilacs drifting from the cemeteries. Emma and I were still up, playing patience, and we glanced up to note smug, blank looks on the hired men's faces. They were privy to some secret. Sitting down at the table, Henry poured a tot of whiskey for himself and one each for Jake and Dennis.

"Now, then, old woman," Henry said, "I have news. We're going to own an automobile." Jake and Dennis studied Emma's face to judge her delight.

"Why would we do that? You don't know how to drive one," she said.

The hired men looked amazed at her response.

"Kolchak'll teach me," Henry said. "Told me so."

"Seems to me we've gotten along pretty well without an automobile. Why throw money away on something we don't need? They're complicated and noisy and they scare the animals."

I could see that the boys wanted to speak up in favor of the automobile, but they kept their mouths shut. The way Jake rolled his eyes, though, it was obviously costing him to stay out of it. I kept out of it, too, though I was as excited as the men.

"Anyway, you said I could get one of those new wash machines," Emma said.

"You can still get a wash machine," Henry told her, though he made the appliance sound as dull as dust, compared to an automobile.

"We're not made of money." Emma folded her hands on the table in a satisfied way, as if to say, "I see I'm the practical one here."

"The crops are planted, the weather's fair, God's in his heaven," Henry said.

"You're the one who always says, don't count the crops till after the harvest," Emma pointed out.

"We can do this," Henry said with assurance and with some impatience. When a man counts on his news being well met and it turns out otherwise, it's a comedown—and a little embarrassing, especially in front of other men, even if they are hired hands. "It's done," he said with finality, and drank the last of his whiskey.

The next day, after church, where Henry broadcast his big news, and after the midday meal, Henry and Emma climbed into the buggy and left for his younger brother Harold's farm, where Henry would further spread the tidings. Emma threw me a "boys will be boys" look as they drove away. I knew from Emma that Harold and Henry were lifelong competitors. The one advantage Harold had was children, four of them, including two boys. But now, Henry was going to own an automobile. So there!

Meanwhile, Dennis, Jake, and Moses set off on the two-mile walk to town to watch the Harvester Hawks' kittenball team play the Red Berry Roosters. The boys had milked the cows before church and I had gathered the eggs, watered the garden, and slopped the hogs, so I was free until evening.

Dennis had caught me after church, asking, "Come to the game? There'll be popcorn and root beer."

"Thank you, but I have letters to write. Maybe another time." The truth was, rather than write to Illinois friends, I simply wanted to laze.

Feeling like a mouse when the cat's away, I carried a kitchen chair to the seldom-used front porch and opened *Godey's Lady's Book*. The afternoon was fine, the air thick and lazy with warmth. Half an hour later, I was so sleepy, the words on the page dimmed, my chin fell to my chest, and *Godey's* dropped to the floor. Retrieving it, I retired to the parlor sofa.

But I woke with a start, swallowing a scream, when someone placed a hand over my mouth and kissed my eyelids. It was Roland. While his fingers fumbled with the buttons of my dress, I began squirming to shed my clothes.

Soon we were thrashing around on the floor. I was naked, my petticoat twisted beneath my hips. Like a starving infant, Roland sought my breasts. What we were doing, I could not say, only that it was agreeable.

Like most girls, I suppose, I had wondered what mating between a man and woman would be like. I'd seen animals coupling but, frankly, had hoped that there might be more to it with humans. And indeed there was: passionate kisses and caresses.

After a bit, Roland groped with his equipment, and seconds later we were achieving a hesitant but juicy coupling, my demanding hands grasping his buttocks. A sharp pain followed, and then a pulsing pleasure that caused my body to rise from my hips. I cried out and then I laughed. In that moment, laughing was a kind of exaltation. Maybe that's what laughing mostly is— exaltation—and maybe that's what mating is too.

As we collapsed like exhausted balloons, I was both happy and sad, but I asked, "May we do it again?" Now Roland laughed, and I laughed once more to hear him.

The meaning of my sadness would slowly dawn: after this afternoon, I could never give myself to Roland for the first time. And after this afternoon, I could never again be the Ruby Drake that I had been.

"Why so quiet?" he asked. "Are you sorry?"

I kissed his neck beneath his ear.

During those two hours, Roland taught me several new words and made me promise never to utter them except with him. And I never have. Time has lent those vulgar words an endearing patina.

When we were done and I had put on my underthings, Roland insisted on fastening the eight nacre buttons on my dress, though his calloused fingers struggled as they had when he'd unbuttoned them. I offered to help, but he brushed my hands aside.

When he'd finished, I kissed the callouses and picked up his shirt to help him into it, but he said, "No," embarrassed perhaps by its shabbiness.

Before he left, Roland said, "Ruby, I don't ever want you to think that what happened was because of Dora or the way she is. What happened was because I love you." He thought for a moment. "There are men who'll tell a girl they love her only because they want to do what we did. That's not the case with us."

Someday, when I was alone and sad, I would open the tapestry bag with the shiny brass closing and hold his words close.

After Roland left and before anyone had returned, I washed out the blood I'd found on my petticoat and hung it up to dry in my room. It pained me to remove the memento.

In late June, the automobile arrived, and after Kolchak had taught Henry the rudiments of it, he spent Sunday afternoons driving the machine in great circles around the farmyard, changing the gears, applying the brakes, honking the horn, and frightening every living thing within half a mile. The sound of the horn alone caused the hens to cut their egg production. Mooing piteously and whinnying nervously, the cows and horses fled to the far end of the pasture. The pigs set up a terrible squealing and wouldn't eat their slop until Henry had returned the automobile to the horse barn at the end of the day. Only Teddy remained calm. After the first circling by the machine, he stood at attention beside the back gate. Whatever inexplicable thing Henry did was all right by his dog.

"It sure does fart a lot," Dennis said of the bang-bang noises the automobile made.

Emma complained daily of the dust it kicked up. One day

she told Henry, "In Lundeen's, a woman said that her nephew broke his arm when he lost control of that crank you start it with. Think of that. Broke his arm." She set her coffee cup down. "When you break your arm, we'll see how much you love that godforsaken thing."

But Henry only smiled and began teaching the boys to drive. I wanted to learn, but Henry said it was "too dangerous for the ladies."

Now and then Roland crossed Cemetery Road to see the automobile, and sometimes Henry gave him a ride around the yard and once even drove them out onto the road itself, turning the machine around in the Protestant cemetery to make the return home. Roland and I were never alone on these occasions, though once he managed to pass me a folded piece of paper, which I thrust into my apron pocket.

Later I read: "Dear Ruby, I think of you all the time. I love you and I don't know what to do. Do you think of me? Try to let me know. Your loving Roland."

I thought about him night and day. But I still took pains not to act moony around Emma. No one could know that Roland and I were lovers. I tried looking ahead, but the future was a dark tunnel with no light at the end.

Now that Henry had his automobile, Emma sat down and ordered a wash machine from Montgomery Ward. The Schoonovers didn't yet have electricity, but lines from town were expected before long. In the meantime we would use it without.

What a to-do the day the machine arrived. Because the wooden crate was large, Kolchak's Dray and Livery picked it up at the Milwaukee depot and brought it out to the farm. And since Henry was an important customer, Arnie Kolchak drove the truck himself, with a shy young helper along to assist.

When they turned into the long drive from Cemetery Road, Teddy ran down to meet them, barking as if we'd been invaded

by the Kaiser's army. Even after Kolchak pulled up to the gate
and turned off the engine, the dog kept running around, barking
and raising more dust than the machine had. While Henry put
Teddy in the horse barn, Emma and I left off our weeding and
headed into the house to pour glasses of iced tea and set out generous slices of devil's food cake on the "good" plates. "They'll
want a break when they're done," she said, adding with a wink,
"Nice-looking boy Kolchak's got with him. 'Hilly Stillman,'
Kolchak said."

Having worked up a sweat setting up the new wash machine
and carrying out the old, Kolchak, Henry, and the boy sat down
at the kitchen table. "Warm day," Henry observed, wiping the
back of his neck with a bandana.

"Sticky too," Kolchak offered.

"Ring around the moon last night," Henry said. "Wouldn't
be surprised if we got rain." And so the timeworn conversation
went, two men at ease with one another.

Later, Kolchak and Hilly rose, donning their caps and thanking Emma. We all followed them out to the gate. As they climbed
into the truck, Henry called out, "Fourth of July, there's a picnic
and dance at the Grange Hall, over by Burmeister's farm. Free
beer. Pack a picnic and come. Mr. Stillman, you're welcome too.
Starts around four." He turned to Emma. "About four, right?"

This was the first I'd heard about a picnic. Surely Roland
would be there. Weeks had passed since I'd seen him, weeks of
wondering if he still felt the same as he'd expressed in the note. I
ached to touch him. At a picnic, a touch was all I could hope for,
but that was better than days of nothing.

No hard frost sneaked in to spoil the garden. The bean and
pea vines were flinging themselves upward, clinging to chicken
wire; the carrot and radish tops bushed out, greener than money;
and the other vegetables, not to be outdone, grew apace. When
we spotted an incursion by rabbits or moles, we plugged up their

opportunities. I toted pails of water from the horse trough till I thought my arms would come loose at the shoulders.

The morning of July Fourth, the peas and beans weren't ready, but I pulled up young carrots, onions, and radishes. From the storm cellar, we picked over last year's potatoes—shriveled and hairy with eyes—selected a few, and cleaned them up for potato salad. Emma killed two hens and we fried them. A jar of watermelon pickles went into the laundry basket, along with gingerbread. "We'll need extra for Roland and Moses," Emma said, adding oatmeal-and-black-walnut cookies to the hamper.

My heart stuttered.

In warm weather, a big galvanized tub leaned against one of the apple trees. If you wanted a real bath, you carried water from the outside pump to fill it. If you drew it early in the day, it warmed up enough for comfort. In the early afternoon I carried a flannel rag, a towel, and soap out to the tub and bathed, leaving no corner unscrubbed. In my room, on the bedside table, was a box of scented talcum and a powder puff I'd bought at the pharmacy. After the bath, I patted myself liberally, trailing the perfume of French Roses through the house as I descended in my best daisy-sprigged muslin dress, a folded note tucked into my pocket.

# CHAPTER EIGHT

The late afternoon was as thick and golden as a jar of honey. Larks soared skyward in bursts of song while mourning doves, in the dense growth hugging the fences, cooed dolefully, recalling old losses.

Serena once told me that after a storm, mourning doves cannot fly until their wings have dried. In this helpless state, they are often attacked by predators, though they huddle together for protection, wings wrapped around one another.

I shrugged these images. No storms threatened the tidy white Grange Hall. Someone, perhaps Moses or Jake or Dennis, had mowed the long grass beneath the giant cottonwoods that shimmied in the breeze. In the purple clover growing deep along the road, bees hummed and hovered, and from all around, cicadas whined. Beyond the fences girding the Hall on three sides, fields of knee-high corn sibilated dryly, and altogether the July afternoon moved and spoke in its own language.

The gentle picture I have painted had been rent by the snort-bang-bang of Henry's automobile as the Schoonovers and I drove up to the Fourth of July picnic. Dennis, Jake, Moses, and Roland were to follow in the sedate old wagon.

Two other automobiles were parked along the road, one Arnie Kolchak's, the other politician John Flynn's. Two horse-drawn wagons, less noisy and without fumes, were allowed to turn in at the gate. The first carried the Harvester Hooligans, a musical group consisting of a fiddle, accordion, saxophone, and comb. The second was adorned with a handsome scroll reading, "Reagan's Saloon and Billiards." The beer had arrived.

Behind the hall, a game of horseshoes was in progress. Old men with hard-won expertise winked slyly to one another, challenging striplings, callow and cocksure of their youth.

Families were making their way on foot into the Grange Hall yard, carrying blankets and baskets of food. These were soon arrayed beneath the trees, woman calling to woman, man hailing man. Little would an outsider guess that as recently as the previous Saturday these same folks had met on Main Street to jaw, trading opinions about rain, rye, corn, and politics.

Four o'clock of a summer afternoon is a pitcher of promise. What but good can pour out? I helped Emma to spread our two quilts side by side on the ground and to unpack picnic gear, but what I wanted to do was dance—polka in the perfume of newly mown grass, run with the children, somersault, sing silly songs, and jump off the Grange Hall steps until someone called, "Now stop that before you break a leg."

At last the hired men arrived from the Schoonover farm. Standing at the open gate, hands in the pockets of their clean overalls, they studied the scene. When I saw Roland, my limbs went watery. I had read of this phenomenon in novels and had figured it was the reaction of flimsy-mimsy girls. Well, I am not the flimsy-mimsy type, and yet my limbs did go watery, so much so that I remained planted on my quilt lest they refuse to support me.

Roland and Dennis sat down on my quilt, Jake and Moses on Emma and Henry's. "On our way, we seen Harold Schoonover and his family coming from the east," Jake told them.

"That's quite a distance for them, just for a picnic," Emma said, bringing out the plates and flatware.

"Maybe they have news," Jake ventured.

"You'd think they'd send a postcard and save themselves the trip," Emma said, a note of chafe in her voice.

"Speak of the devil." Henry pointed to the gate where his brother and his brother's family stood as the boys had done minutes earlier, surveying the crowd until they spied us.

Waving and calling, they came on, spreading quilts directly across the lawn from us. The tall sons and two little girls wandered off to join other youngsters playing tag. From their quilts, Harold's wife, Hermione, waved a handkerchief as Harold crossed to us.

"Hermy's expecting," Harold said. "It's early days, but she don't like to go out after she starts to show, so we decided to come while we could. And, by gum," he said to Henry, "I wanted to tell you how glad I am you came over that day to talk about ordering an automobile. We got to thinking we should too. Kolchak says it'll be here in maybe three weeks."

Henry was standing now. "That so?"

Emma leaned toward me, hissing, "*Hermy* could be carrying triplets, and it'd never show." Emma was upset. Harold had gone right out and bought an automobile after Henry had. "Jack Spratt and his wife."

Indeed, Harold, like Henry, was as lean as a hoe handle. Both men were attractive in a weathered sort of way, like Emma. It was, I'd decided, a special kind of beauty—like that of things hard-used but strong and carved right down to their foundations.

Beneath her breath, Emma said, "I 'spose we'd better go say hello, since she's not going to get up off her tuffet." She took my hand and we stood. "Hermione," she called to her sister-in-law, without enthusiasm.

"Emma," Hermione returned, her voice likewise lacking a note of happy expectation.

Drawing close, Emma said, "Hermione, this is our hired girl, Ruby. More like a daughter." Without letting go of my hand, Emma held me at arm's length, putting me on display. "Pretty as a picture," she said and drew me back again. "Harold tells us you're expecting. When're you due?"

"Around Christmas, Dr. White says." In a preening gesture, Hermione smoothed a strand of hair into the nest of fat curls on her head. "Number five."

"You're feeling good?"

"Like a million dollars. Harold says I'm bloomin'."

"Hoping for a girl or boy?"

"Well, naturally we'd like another boy. Helpful on a farm."

"Tell you the truth, I wouldn't trade Ruby for half a dozen boys. Brains. It takes brains to make a farm run good." Emma gazed off toward a horizon of slim hopes. "Well, I expect we'd better get food laid out for the men. Nice to see you, Hermione."

We returned to our side of the yard, Emma saying, "I *do* dislike that woman. Why is that?" Then, "And don't you dare tell me why, Ruby." She laughed at her own naked need. She so wanted a son.

Roland lay on his side, propped up on one elbow, the breeze ruffling his hair. A pain in my chest warned me of I knew not what.

He smiled a smile that said, "We have a secret," and I returned it, but knew that in mine there was sadness I could not filter.

"Roland, may I fill a plate for you?" I asked, keeping my voice light.

"Anytime. Anywhere," he said, his voice teasing, but his look intense.

When I handed him a plate, I passed him the note from my pocket as well. *Darling Roland*, it read, *I love you with all my heart. I long to touch you. Yours, R.* With a slight nod, and without opening it, he slipped the note discreetly into one of the pockets on the front of his overalls.

For a while, the seven of us sat eating and chatting, though truthfully, I didn't do much of either. When we had finished, Emma and I rinsed off the plates at the pump beside the Grange Hall steps. Descending those same steps was a gentleman with a look of well-being, even affluence. His sleeves were rolled above the elbows, and his collar was loosened. He smiled at us and when he reached the ground, he removed his panama hat and made a slight bow to Emma. She set down the plate she was rinsing, wiped her hands on her skirt, and offered her hand to him.

"Mrs. Schoonover," he said, "Keeping well?"

"Very well, Congressman. And you?"

"Never better." Surveying the picnic, he said, "Grand gathering. I don't have many opportunities to see old friends these days. I was darned pleased when Henry invited me."

"Congressman, this is our good hired girl, Ruby Drake."

He took my hand, saying, "An honor."

"Have you eaten?" Emma asked. "We've got plenty."

"Thank you, but I ate before I came. More time to visit." He cast a look around. "Henry's here?"

"By the beer wagon, I wouldn't be surprised."

"I'll say hello." He took Emma's hand once more, then returned the hat to his head and moved away from us.

"John Flynn," Emma explained to me. "Congressman. The only Democrat Henry votes for." Our dishes rinsed, we returned to the quilts to find the men had indeed wandered off to the beer wagon, while the Harvester Hooligans were tuning up as twilight crept over the scene.

Since it was the Fourth of July, the Hooligans launched the

evening with "The Stars and Stripes Forever," bravely rendered, considering the limitations of their four instruments. Much whistling and clapping followed. Immediately the quartet settled into "My Wild Irish Rose," and we women and girls sang along.

And now it was "Down by the Old Mill Stream." Babies on their blankets grew drowsy while older brothers and sisters, at their mothers' scolding, found quiet games to pursue.

The evening star emerged in the pale sky, then another and another. In the deepening dusk, larks continued erupting into the air, like gentle fireworks, enjoying lyrical last hurrahs. For a moment, their song undid me. "What is it?" Emma asked.

I shook my head. "Nothing. Just the larks." Emma didn't inquire as to my meaning. She was the kind of woman who could nod and let it go.

A number of men, borrowing a couple of tables from inside the Grange Hall, set up card games beyond the beer wagon. All around the yard, women hung kerosene lanterns on fence posts, each casting a gay circle of light. I felt trapped between the good cheer of the lantern glow and the darkness of the universe.

Possibly to lift my spirits, Emma told me, "Pretty soon there'll be dancing, out there in the middle of the yard. I expect you'll be asked."

I remembered how Serena and Denton had loved to dance. It required only a scrap of music to get them on their feet—Mrs. Bullfinch launching into "Vilia," or the band in the park playing "Meet Me In St. Louis, Louis"—and Denton would grasp Serena's waist and whisk her away, her long skirt eddying around her legs.

We had no carpet in our dining room so Denton swept Serena round and round the dining table while I lay on the sofa watching, enchanted. They were a prince and princess, and the Palace Ball was whirling giddily across our dining room, Denton's eyes shining, Serena's cheeks glowing.

More and more I missed them, Serena especially, as they floated away from me on a stream of passing time. Never had I felt more alone than in this pale blue hour, in the midst of human company and "Down by the Old Mill Stream."

# CHAPTER NINE

At nine, the sky was loath to relinquish the last remnants of day. In the semidarkness, some couples had begun dancing in the center of the yard, others indoors where the windows were thrown open. Between these windows, a handful of old women sat straight-backed along the walls, observing and nodding, even as they tatted or knitted caps and mittens for the coming winter. Ahead, always, the long winter.

In the yard, I found my way past the blankets and quilts to the back of the building where four old men, as wrinkled as raisins, still hurled horseshoes with some accuracy despite the gloaming. Two outhouses beckoned, each with a lighted lamp.

When I returned to the Schoonover quilts, Roland was dancing a schottische with Emma. An awful jealousy seized me.

When they returned to our quilt, Emma's hair coming undone, and when the music struck up again, Roland approached me and held out his hand. I rose as the saxophone eased into the third or fourth bar of "Moonlight Bay."

The song was slow enough that we had breath to talk—or,

rather, Roland had. I had neither breath nor words, only a suffocating physical need.

"I wish we could be alone," he said.

I nodded. Finally, I said, "I . . . I want to swallow you."

Now *he* nodded.

"That way, you'd always be with me."

"I wish I had good words," he said. "At night in bed or . . . when I'm out in the field, I think of things to say. But when I see you or write a note, the words go away."

"Your words are lovely. They're yours." I squeezed his hand. He tried to pull me closer, but we could not dance that way, not here in front of people who knew us. "Oh, God, oh, God," I whispered and started to cry.

"What's wrong?"

The question was so silly, I laughed. What was *wrong*? I shook my head. "So many things."

He gripped my waist tightly, and then "Moonlight Bay" was ending, almost before it had begun.


Back at the quilt, Henry was telling Emma, "They're talkin' war at the beer wagon. Flynn says he's against it, but he ain't sure it won't happen."

"War with Germany? Oh Lord, no. I hate the thought of it," Emma said, twisting her hair tightly back into its usual knot high on her head.

Returning from his own trip to the beer wagon, Dennis overheard. "I wouldn't mind cleaning the Kaiser's clock," he said.

"Oh, don't talk smart," Emma scolded. "I don't want to think about you going over there."

"Well, my dad says it's a sure thing, and it won't matter how Flynn votes, it's gonna happen. Look what they did to the *Lusitania*."

"Yes," Emma admitted. "Those poor Lundeens." She shook her head.

With his "smart" talk, which was not at all like him, I wondered if Dennis had enjoyed one too many jars of beer. He moved soberly enough, and he didn't slur his words, but when he asked me to dance, his eyes were bold. If I refused him, though, it would look strange. Tread lightly. Emma was no fool.

The accordion wheezed into "By the Light of the Silvery Moon" and Dennis grabbed my hand. He danced well, not like someone tipsy. But then he said, "You were making googly eyes at Roland." Those words had required Dutch courage.

I felt the starch go out of me. "What do you mean?"

"It's like . . . you *like* him."

I stiffened. My insides pushed up against my spine. I tried to sound casual. "I do like him. I think he's nice, don't you?"

"He's all right."

"Just 'all right'?"

"Well, don't you ever wonder about that wife of his, why she doesn't show herself? What's that about?"

"What do you *think* it's about?"

"Maybe he doesn't treat her right. Or maybe she thinks he's . . . straying, and she's embarrassed."

"I think she hasn't gotten over losing the baby."

"After all this time?"

"Losing a baby must be a terrible thing for a woman."

"Then it'd be a terrible thing if he was straying."

"What makes you so sure he's straying?"

"I'm *not* sure. But I see the way he looks at you, and I saw you pass him something this afternoon."

I don't know how I managed not to trip over my feet. "Oh, *that*," I said scornfully. "It was just a funny poem I found in one of Henry's old farm journals."

"Well . . . just remember, Roland Allen's spoken for."

In town the thunder of fireworks began. I looked at the quilt. "If you're done insulting me, I'm going to watch the fireworks," I said, breaking away and hurrying back to Emma and Henry.

But I hardly noticed the fireworks as I sat with the others. My face still flamed. Was Dennis jealous of Roland? What if he shared his suspicions with Emma or Henry? Worse, what if he went to Dora? As the fireworks wound down to a final burst of pop-pop-pops and I packed up the picnic, the beautiful night had soured.

"Roland, come with us in the automobile," Emma said. "I know you like a ride."

Across the yard, the Harold Schoonover children were packing up while the parents lingered, shooting the breeze with another family. Minutes later, our party followed theirs to the gate, where Hermione turned to trill, "Next year at this time, we'll have our new automobile—and maybe a new son too!"


In the dark back seat of Henry's Model T, there was no way to talk above the noise of the machine without shouting. I couldn't warn Roland about Dennis. Reflecting on his words, I shivered. Mistaking the trembling, Roland chafed my hands to warm them.

We kissed. He caressed my breasts through the fabric of my dress and I laid a hand between his legs. How melancholy this happiness was.

# CHAPTER TEN

O n the day following the picnic, after the noon meal, Emma and I were working in the garden tying tomato plants to stakes.

As Emma sat back on her haunches, wiping perspiration from her temples with a flannel cloth, Teddy suddenly set up a tune and went running down the drive toward Cemetery Road. As we started for the gate, Moses came running up the long drive, panting and calling as best he could.

Our men were in the field, preparing for a second hay crop, so Emma and I ran to meet the old man. Moses was breathing hard and holding his side.

"Moses, what is it?" Emma asked. "Get your wind."

Wild-eyed, he shook his head, unable to get the words out. Finally, leaning heavily on the back gate, he wheezed, "Mrs. Allen . . . fell in the barn."

"Is she hurt bad?"

He could only nod again and again, pointing back the way he'd come.

"Where's Roland?"

"Gone for the doctor," he breathed.

"Ruby and I'll go. You take your time," she told him. We gathered up our skirts and dashed down the drive.

The wide barn door was open, as it had been the day I'd found Roland there. Still in her nightgown, Dora lay on a bed of straw. Her right leg was twisted strangely, and she was moaning and sobbing and nursing her right arm.

"Roland has gone for the doctor," Emma told her. "Can we make you more comfortable?"

Dora shook her head.

"Ruby and I'll stay with you till Roland gets back." She handed Dora a clean handkerchief. "How'd this happen?"

"Naaah," Dora cried, drawing the word out in a long lamentation, as if not only pain but some awful regret were being wrung from her.

Emma glanced around. I followed her gaze when it stopped. Hanging from a rafter was a length of rope with a badly constructed noose at one end. Leaning beside it was a rough ladder, probably the one used to climb to the hay mow. Emma looked at me and shook her head. Though the day was July hot, Dora had begun to twitch and shiver. "Get a blanket from the house," Emma said.

When I returned, Roland was just turning in at the drive. Behind his wagon came a buggy carrying Dr. White and his nurse. The pain in Roland's face as he leapt from the wagon was wrenching. He was full of guilt, as was I. But—so cold was my heart—I still thought, I love you as much as before.

Dr. White carried a folded stretcher, and the nurse followed with his bag. The doctor nodded to us, then told Emma, "Leave us, Mrs. Schoonover. We'll get her into the house. No doubt you'll be needed later."

As Emma and I headed toward the Allens' back door, I looked over my shoulder to see the doctor holding a cloth to Dora's face. Her crying died away.

Inside the house, I followed Emma up the stairs to prepare the bedroom. A scene of domestic warfare met us: a wedding photo, wrested from the wall, had been thrown to the floor, its glass broken; brush, comb, and other articles of toilette were swept from the top of a bureau; clothing, Roland's and Dora's, was scattered like bits of tornado refuse; even the bedclothes were flung into a muddle.

"Run across the road and bring back clean sheets and pillowcases," Emma said. "Take these with you to be washed." She gathered up the linens from the bed, shoving them into my arms.

When I returned with the bedding, Emma had put the room in order and swept up the glass. The wedding photo had disappeared. We made up the bed quickly when we heard the doctor and Roland carrying Dora into the house and up the stairs. Then Emma and I moved into the hall, giving the men room to maneuver. The doctor came first, Roland holding his end of the stretcher high to keep Dora level. The nurse followed.

When Dora lay in bed, straight as a corpse, the doctor told Roland, Emma, and me, "Leave us be for a few minutes. I'm going to set the bones."

Heading back downstairs to wait, we sat at the kitchen table, silent, Roland pale, shaking his head, trying, I knew, to sort out what was happening; Emma preoccupied, kneading her hands as if applying balm.

Twenty minutes later, Dr. White and the nurse joined us. "I'll be back tomorrow early to put a cast on the leg and arm. In the meantime, she should sleep. With any luck, through the night. Don't let her toss. She probably won't. She's knocked out for now." Turning to Roland, he said, "If she wakes and the pain is bad, give her two teaspoons of this." The nurse handed him his bag and he reached into it for a brown bottle, handing it to Roland.

When they had left, Emma told Roland, "I'll drive the wagon

over with our commode. Dora won't be able to take the stairs or use the chamber pot for a while." Leave it to dear Emma to think of such practicalities. Roland nodded though I wasn't sure he heard or understood.

Rising, she laid a hand on his shoulder and, in a strange, tender voice, said, "We'll get through this, buckaroo." She patted him, and we left, but not before she added, "Ruby and I'll bring supper over. We'll all eat here tonight, our men too."

The afternoon was ebbing as we hurried back across the road.

"Do you think she left a note?" I asked Emma.

"I didn't see one."

"What about the doctor? Do you think the doctor noticed the rope?"

"Yes."

"Will he tell? Will there be scandal?"

"He won't tell."

"And the nurse?"

"Sarah Gilmore won't tell."

"How can you be sure?"

"He's a good man." Emma paused for breath and to wipe her face on her sleeve. "And years ago Sarah's daughter walked into the lake late one night after her beau threw her over. It was a scandal, all right. The daughter was buried outside the cemetery fence, mind you. The boy hanged himself a few months later." We set out again. "There's more of this goes on than you might think."


After the supper dishes were washed and the Allen kitchen tidied, Emma and I prepared to head home. The men, who were sitting on the back steps smoking, rose to let us pass. Henry told Emma, "You go ahead. I'll be along."

Emma turned to Roland. "In the morning, Ruby'll come over and stay with Dora. You can't afford to take a day off."

Later, in my room, I finally had time to think, though it curdled the dinner inside me. Pacing the length of my room, I wondered if Dora had tried to hang herself because of Roland and me. If so, how had she found out? Dennis hadn't had time to do mischief. And anyway, I wasn't sure he was the sort. He might be jealous or protective, but he wasn't a villain.

And if Dora *had* by some means found out, what would happen tomorrow when I began caring for her? Even lying broken and in pain, she was bound to be murderously angry. I would be.

And would Dora tell Emma? And would I be sent packing? I didn't really fear *that*. I could make my way somehow. It was losing Emma and Roland that I feared. What must Roland be enduring? I hoped that Dora slept through the night. Even so, how could Roland sleep, maybe ever again, with questions like these chewing his insides?

You may notice that I have made no mention of what Dora was feeling, beyond anger—her sorrow, her humiliation. No, all my worries centered on Roland and myself, the damage she could inflict on us.

I held the photograph of Serena and Denton to my heart. What would Serena say about all of this? Would she call me a monster? *Was* I a monster?

Serena and Denton had never talked about "sin." On the other hand, Aunt Bertha had talked a good deal about it. To hear her tell it, sin was at the heart of nearly everything—certainly everything that was enjoyable.

If I understood the meaning of sin, Roland and I were surely up to our necks in it. Perhaps I *was* a monster.

# CHAPTER ELEVEN

"You best get over there before the doctor leaves. Likely he'll have instructions. Take a sandwich," Emma said, thrusting one at me. Though we'd been late rising this morning, the sun wasn't fully above the horizon.

"I haven't set the table for breakfast," I said.

"Go. I saw the doctor's buggy. And take some rags for cleaning."

And so I went, dragging my heels, wondering how yesterday's domestic war at the Allens' had begun. If I was the cause, was Roland sorry he'd ever laid eyes on me? No matter, I would still love him. I might be seventeen, but there are things you know, granite-hard *know*, even at seventeen.

The day was hot with thick, heavy air that pressed on scalp and shoulders. My head weighed fifty pounds, and I lugged my body across the road like a gunny sack of potatoes. Except for a hawk sailing slowly back and forth across the sky searching for breakfast, even the birds were quiet, conserving energy. The dust of the road, given to flushing upward at the smallest disturbance, barely troubled itself on this dense morning.

The farmyard was silent. Lying in the shade of the rock elm, panting, Red noted my arrival with a lazy wave of his feathery tail, but didn't rise. I filled his battered tin bowl with water and slouched into the house.

The night before, Emma had said, "I want you to spend your days with Dora. Roland's barely hanging on to that place. He can't afford to bring in a hired woman. You'll be a great help to him."

"But what'll *you* do?"

"I know a woman from town I can get temporary."

Now I sat down at Roland's table, pecking without interest at my sandwich. I supposed that Roland was upstairs with the doctor and nurse. When he came down, what would his face tell me?

Had he eaten breakfast? I set aside my sandwich and found one of Emma's loaves in the bread box. When had she delivered that? Only now was I glimpsing how much Roland meant to her, the pain and concern she must be feeling. And if she learned that I was at the bottom of his troubles, dear God. My fears chased each other.

At length, I grabbed a basket from beside the back door and went to gather eggs. Moses had milked the cows and was letting them out to pasture. Had he heard yesterday's battle? If so, what did he make of it? Emma had said that Moses was as devoted to Roland as he was to the Roman church.

An orphan from "back east," Moses had decades ago worked his way across the country, ending up as a farmhand. "He's taken to the work body and soul," Emma told me. "He certainly took to Roland like a son."

"And he never had a . . . lady friend?" I asked.

"I can't speak to that," Emma said, "though I did hear that

Mrs. Hartwell, the priest's housekeeper, has been a good friend over the years."


Followed by Roland, nurse Gilmore and Dr. White finally descended the stairs, the nurse folding a rubber sheet, the doctor telling Roland, "Keep her quiet and immobile today. Tomorrow she can use the commode, but she'll need help. Meanwhile, the bedpan."

He turned to me. "You'll be here?"

"Yes."

"You heard what I told Mr. Allen. She can have food and liquids, no dietary restrictions. Keep her entertained and quiet as best you can. She's riled." He shook hands with Roland, and was gone, the nurse with him.

Now that we were alone, I didn't know what to say. But at length, "Have you had breakfast?"

"A cup of coffee." Shoulders hunched, he looked at me from beneath his brows, as if he feared I might hurl something at him.

"I'll make eggs and toast." What a pitiful pair we were. Desperate to know what the other was thinking, yet dreading to know, each of us feeling small when measured against the enormity of what had occurred.

"I shouldn't take time to sit."

"Don't be silly. Anyway, I've got questions." My hands trembled as I reached for eggs from the basket.

We were silent for the ten minutes required to prepare a plate of eggs and toast, and reheat coffee. Drawing out a chair opposite him, I asked, "What happened yesterday morning?" My voice seemed to come from another room. It sounded older, like some other woman's.

"Well, we had a row."

"What about?"

"She said I didn't love her. That I was sneaking around with somebody. She'd felt it for a long time, she said, but now she had proof.

"I asked her what she meant by that, but she started screaming and beating on me. I let her. I figured I owed her that. 'Don't pretend,' she said. Then she began to throw things and get crazy. After a while she went limp and got . . . quiet." He looked at his coffee cup, but didn't pick it up. "She never said she was going to kill herself."

I sat frozen, waiting.

"The thing was, I couldn't make myself deny any of it or . . . or tell her I loved her. I don't think I could've done that, even if she'd said she was going to do what she did." His voice drained of energy, he asked, "What are you thinking?"

"When I look at you, I get dizzy-crazy." He smiled, a little miracle. "But, to tell the truth, I don't see a happy ending," I said. He started to say something, but I interrupted, "Right at this minute, I'm feeling grown-up. While it lasts, I'm going to make a rule: as long as I'm in Dora's house, we will not touch each other."

"Why? That day in the barn, we were touching each other."

"That was different."

"How?"

"I don't know exactly, but it was. This rule is something I *feel*, not something I understand."

He grunted, shaking his head. "If I can't abide by it?"

"You'll have to, if you want me to help out here." The effort to say these words exhausted me. He finished breakfast in silence and headed to work. I slumped at the table, the starch in my spine oozing away.

From above came Dora's voice, "Who's down there?"

With trepidation, I climbed the stairs. How would I keep Dora calm, as the doctor had ordered, if she knew about Roland and me?

"I'm here," I said, clearing my throat and stepping into the bedroom, tiptoeing, the way you do entering a sick room. My hands were dug into my apron pockets to quiet them. "Would you like some breakfast?"

Beneath a loose gown, Dora's right arm and leg were in casts. Her long blonde hair fell in soft waves around a wan face dominated by enormous pale blue eyes. In a small voice, she said, ". . . just toast and coffee, if there is any."

"Cream and sugar?"

"Cream."

She was sending out waves of different emotions, chief among them embarrassment. Two vivid splotches appeared on her cheeks. Suicide was a scandal, especially in a small rural community and especially if you didn't succeed. If you succeeded, well, what did you *care*?

Added to this was the certain knowledge that some people would know why she'd done it, and the rest would guess that her husband was catting around. And she the town beauty. Her fists were balled tightly on the bed beside her.

I would truly have liked to spare her this, but I was obliged to be with her, wait on her, and who knew for how long? The least I could do was pretend I knew nothing. It might save her a crumb of self-respect.

"No egg?"

"No egg."

Headed back down the stairs, I realized she didn't know about me. So what had been her "proof"?

After I prepared a fresh pot of coffee and set it on the stove, I flew out to the yard, up the drive, and along the fence, looking for a flower or two. I was ecstatic that she didn't suspect me. More generously, I wanted to give her a spot of beauty on the worst day of her life. I found a scraggly stand of wild daisies. They wouldn't last—wildflowers never did—but they were something bright.

Back in the kitchen, I arranged them in a mason jar and set them on a makeshift tray, a big cake pan lined with a napkin.

Slathering Emma's apple butter on the toast, I poured plenty of cream into the coffee, and headed back up the stairs, my tread lighter than earlier.

When I had helped Dora with her toast and coffee, she looked at me almost shyly and asked, "Who are you?"

I was wary. Was this a trick question? "I'm Emma and Henry's hired girl, Ruby." I moved the tray to the chifforobe.

"I mean, where do you come from?"

"Illinois."

"And how did you get to this godforsaken part of the world?"

Given her pain and our general circumstances, this seemed an odd conversation, though maybe any small distraction was better than a knowing silence. I explained about Serena and Denton.

"What happened then, after they died?"

Then had come the Osters in Iowa and, after that, the Schoonovers and Harvester.

"A lot of life."

If our strange little conversation was diverting her from pain and humiliation, I would linger over details, like Mrs. Bullfinch and Professor Cromwell, her singing, his inventions. She smiled at Mrs. Bullfinch and the commercial travelers. "Mr. Cromwell sounds like a lovely man," she said. "He'll go far." She nodded to herself.

I didn't want her comparing him with Roland, to Roland's disadvantage, so I hurried on. "Aunt Bertha was another story." I described the lace curtains, washed, starched, and stretched, spring and fall, and how I mustn't touch them because my hands were either damp or dirty.

"She hated deep summer because southern Illinois is humid then, and the curtains went limp. If you touched them, they felt sticky. I think the starch had sugar in it. In secret, I crunched them in my fists, even though I didn't like the way they felt. I just *had* to because she didn't want me to. If she'd been kind, I would never have touched them. Do you understand?"

She nodded and attempted to rearrange herself on the bed. The heat in the second floor room was oppressive and, combined with the casts, would be an increasing aggravation. I recalled one July when Mrs. Bullfinch had tripped on the porch steps and fallen.

"Can I help?"

She shook her head.

"What would you like for lunch?"

"I won't be hungry."

"I'll see what's in the icebox."

As I started from the room, she said, "Thank you, Ruby. You're a kind person."

*Oh, Dora.*

# CHAPTER TWELVE

A round ten a.m. that morning, Emma showed up at the back door, holding down her straw hat against the hot west wind that swept grit from the farmyard into her hair and eyes. "I've got a beef roast and vegetables on the stove," she said, collapsing onto a kitchen chair and fanning herself with the hat. "When they're ready, I'll fetch 'em across."

"You've got enough on your hands over there," I said. "I can find something here."

"And you've got enough on your hands here," she said, laughing. "How is she?"

I sat down. "I don't know. She's in pain, but she's quiet, humiliated. It's . . . it's like a strange calm between storms. Eerie."

Emma stood and crossed to the stove to lay a hand on the cold coffeepot. She grabbed a tin mug and filled it from the bucket beside the kitchen pump. After first drinking half the water in the mug, she soaked a handkerchief in what remained and wiped her face. "That's better." Hanging the handkerchief over the back of a chair to dry, she asked, "Did she say anything to you about that business?" Emma stretched her long arm toward the barn.

"No. She asked who I was, where I came from." I reheated the coffee yet again. "Will you say hello while you're here?"

"Tomorrow. Today, she's gonna be too embarrassed. She knows I never approved of the marriage. And now, this." Emma studied her hands, the nails split and broken, the knuckles red.

"I mean, I never said anything to her," Emma went on, "but she knew. She was the kinda girl who never had anything in her head but whether the sash on her dress matched the ribbon in her hair. I used to tell Henry the only reason she walked downtown was to remind folks how pretty she was.

"And a'course, when Roland came to town, he was every bit as pretty as she was. I think she set her cap for him the minute he stepped off the train."

I poured the reheated coffee into her mug and fetched a clean spoon and the cream pitcher.

Emma nodded her thanks, stirred the coffee, and tasted it. "Who made this?"

"Roland."

She smiled. "Just the way I like it. You could stand a brick on it." She was silent for a minute, then: "I don't *dis*like her. I just don't *like* her. She was never good enough for Roland. If he loses the farm, I'll always blame her."

"How did he come by the farm?" I asked, pouring myself a cup and sitting across from Emma.

"Old Mr. Allen, his dad's older brother, had homesteaded it. But he was never in real good health. Bad lungs. Roland was sent to help out, but then the uncle passed on and left it to him, and it came with a passel of debts. Machinery and such. Still, Roland's half-killed himself holding on, bless his heart."

She sighed, leaning back and closing her eyes. "That one," she said, tilting her head to indicate Dora, "is like some falderal piece of jewelry. Pretty, but not good for much." She spooned more sugar into her coffee. "She tried to play house when she came out to the farm, but she doesn't know *how*."

"Good thing Moses hangs on."

"Stays on out of the goodness of his heart. I think Mrs. Hartwell would like to take him in, but he worries about Roland." She sighed again. "What's to be done?" The persistent question.

I thought I knew her well enough to ask, "Roland's like your son, isn't he?"

She teared up, nodding fiercely and reaching for the drying handkerchief. "Damn her." Rising, she said, "I'd best be going."

"I didn't mean to hurt you," I told her.

"Don't worry, little girl. I'll be fine." Grabbing her hat, she was gone.


After the men had eaten their midday meal, I went outside to cut more wildflowers for Dora's tray. A merciless sun painted wet mirages on surfaces where there was neither dew nor rain. Perspiration ran down my legs and back, making them itch. My eyes burned from salt oozing out of my hairline. I wiped my legs with my petticoat, my forehead with my apron. I loved sun and heat, but people were meant to put their feet up on a chaise and drink iced tea on days like this one.

Back in Beardsley, Serena spent the muggy southern Illinois mornings attending summer classes at the college. While she studied *Beowulf* or Shakespeare's tragedies, I toted a basket of books and puzzles next door to Mrs. Bullfinch's backyard to occupy myself.

But when Serena returned at noon, she cobbled together lunch from thick slices of bread with salami and sliced radishes or cheese and pickles, carrying the sandwiches into the yard, along with glasses of iced tea from the big pitcher in the icebox.

Then Serena sat back on a ratty old rattan chaise while I crossed my legs Indian-style on the quilt beside her. And when we had eaten every crumb and drunk every drop of iced tea, Serena read to me from whatever she'd been studying that morning. In the middle of the reading, we would fall asleep in the palmy, buzzing shade.

When I carried up the tray with a cup of Emma's beef broth and toast, Dora had thrown off the top sheet and was fanning herself with a paper fan from the Seed and Feed store.

"I'm not hungry," she said. Little wonder with the heat, but I was determined to see her well. If I'd been the cause of her accident, I wasn't going to be the cause of her wasting.

Unlike earlier, Dora was remote now, turning her head away and peering at me askance. As I helped her to drink the broth, she asked, with some petulance, "Where'd this come from?" If I were caught in a miasma of heat, pain, and humiliation, I supposed I'd be petulant too.

"Emma brought it over. She also brought a beef roast for the men."

"I've had better broth."

"Have you? When was that?" I didn't like her slurring Emma.

Dora shrugged. Afterward, I helped her with the bedpan and was thankful for Emma's rubber pad which kept the spillage from wetting the bottom sheet. Still, for Dora, the whole maneuver was painful, awkward, and embarrassing, especially in front of a strange girl.

"Tomorrow you'll be able to use the commode," I told her.

"Who said?"

"Dr. White."

"We'll see," she peeved.

Though shaded by the rock elm outside the window, the bedroom was nevertheless stifling. We swam in our own staleness. I supposed that Dora was perspiring beneath the casts. That would be torture.

"Does your leg itch?" I asked. "Would you like me to bring up a spirea switch? You could scratch it under the cast."

"Suit yourself," she snapped. *Suit yourself.* All right, I won't bring one, then, and you can stew in your own juices.

I carried the damp rubber pad downstairs and returned for the tray, setting the jar of daisies beside the bed. "I have to do the dishes and clean up the kitchen now," I told her, "but if you'd like company later, I'll come up."

"I'll call if I want you." She tried to turn onto her side, away from me, but was unsuccessful. Instead, she pulled the sheet up, a sheet she didn't need, and set her face to the wall.

With my chores out of the way, I wandered outside again and around the scruffy, unkempt yard. At the southwest corner of the house, someone had planted vegetables. Moses? Bedraggled and dusty, they were parched, so I began hauling buckets of water from the trough.

North of the little garden, the rock elm, shielding Dora and Roland's bedroom with drooping, graceful branches, shivered and soughed dryly. How pleasant it would be to lie naked in that bed at night, listening to the sighing of the leaves.

When I carried up the midday tray, Dora pretended to be asleep, so I set the tray on the chifforobe and stood at the window watching the elm dance. I swayed a little to its rhythm.

"What are you doing?" she asked.

I didn't turn. "I'm swaying."

"Why are you here?"

"I brought up your tray. There's soft-boiled egg and toast, and I cooked some new little carrots."

"I meant why are you here in my house?" Her tone was both dramatic and dismissive.

I turned. "Emma said I was needed. She said Roland can't farm and also look after you. And he can't afford a hired woman. He's barely hanging onto this place."

"Nosy Emma again. And really, Ruby, it's no skin off your nose if he can't hang on."

Heat rising in my cheeks, I stared at her for a long minute. *She's in pain. She's mortified.*

But what she'd said set me thinking. What if Roland lost the farm and they moved away? Then Dora wouldn't have to face Harvester. "Is that what you're hoping?" I asked. "That Roland will lose the farm?"

Two days ago Dora had tried to hang herself, and here I was pestering her. No wonder she was cross. My heart must be as dark and hard as a black walnut. Still, I asked again, "Is that what you're hoping?" I thought I caught a glint of guilt in her eyes.

"Leave me alone!"


While I scrubbed the kitchen floor, I heard Dora pounding on the wall. Drying my hands on my apron, I headed back upstairs, carrying the clean, dry rubber pad.

"Yes?" I asked, stepping into the bedroom and noting that she had eaten what I'd brought earlier.

"I need the bedpan," she said, not the least note of "please" in her voice.

"Well, lift up your rear so I can get this pad under you," I told her, no conciliation in mine.

She was better at the maneuvering than before, and we managed to keep the pad dry. I left with the bedpan in one hand, the tray in the other, and no further word spoken. Florence Nightingale I wasn't.

Several days passed like this, me trying to make allowances for her pain and disgrace, her angry because of that pain and disgrace. I waited longer than the doctor had suggested before demanding that Dora use the commode.

"I hate the commode," she said.

"And you hate the bedpan. Maybe you can just hold the pee until you're up and about," I joked unkindly, wheeling the commode to the bedside.

Though I tried to help her lift the leg that was weighted with the cast, she made a great to-do of getting herself to the edge of the bed. Hobbling on her good leg, she pivoted and flopped onto the commode, yipping with pain and banging the arm cast against the chair. Everything was a grand production. Or perhaps it seemed that way because I'd taken a dislike to her—though perhaps I ought to divide my dislike by six, given that I loved her husband.

One day, after about a week, I carried up a tray, telling her, "I killed a couple of chickens, so you and the men can have a nice meal with potatoes and gravy. And there's some new little onions."

"You really *are* a hired girl, aren't you?" She'd been thinking about this. She studied her nails, buffed recently.

"What do you mean?"

"I mean you were cut out for this business: killing chickens, milking cows. Fetching and carrying." Her voice wasn't nasty, but matter-of-fact.

I found myself bristling. At the same time, I was proud of being able to kill a chicken and milk a cow. Still, I wanted to be thought of as a hired girl who also spoke proper English and could recite a bit of poetry, if called upon.

"Yes, I suppose I am cut out for this business," I said. "But I'm cut out for plenty more as well."

Scorn, or what passed for it, was undisguised in her glance. "And what would that be?" If she'd been brought low, at least she wouldn't be patronized by a hired girl.

My temper pinched me hard. "Well, one thing I'm not cut out for is lying in bed, swilling quack medicine and sleeping my life away because someone spoiled me till I'm good for nothing."

I grabbed the tray off the chifforobe and thrust it on the bed. "When you need to pee, pound on the wall. Maybe I'll come."

"I'm going to tell Roland how you treat me," she yelled after me as I descended the stairs.

"I'll tell him myself."

And so I did, at supper. I didn't care that Moses was sitting at the table, hearing every word. "She knows how to get under my skin," I said, passing the potatoes and gravy around.

"I'm sorry to hear it," Roland said. "Pay no attention. She's like that." Forking up a chicken leg and glancing sidelong at me, he smiled. "Sounds like you give as good as you get."

For the first time in days, we all laughed.


Roland was meant to be a farmer. Yes, he'd had other dreams, but he did love this small, debt-ridden place. You could hear it in the mealtime talk between him and Moses. You could see it in the way he gave himself without complaint to the heavy work of it.

Probably most people had more than one path they could happily follow. If I were his wife, maybe he'd have time in the evening to read history. And if we had children—and we would—he could entertain them with stories of Socrates and Julius Caesar, the pharaohs and Alexander the Great. If I were Roland's wife.

# CHAPTER THIRTEEN

M ost evenings, when the dinner dishes were put away, I walked across Cemetery Road alone or Emma came to meet me. This evening, Roland grabbed a broken spade handle from beside the back door, saying, "I'll walk you home. There's been a wild dog prowling the road the last few nights. You can hear him howling after dark."

"How do you know it's a 'him'?"

"Well, I suppose I don't. Could be a bitch."

"Where do wild dogs come from?"

"Maybe folks pass through and dump 'em. Maybe the owner dies. Whatever it was, this one's lost his people."

As we walked up his drive toward the road, he said, "I put Red in the barn. Tell Henry to watch Teddy, keep the gate closed at night. Our dogs might try to follow, especially if it's a female."

Though the sky was still light at eight-thirty, he held my hand, as if to protect me. I knew I ought to unclasp myself, but I also knew that Dora couldn't see us through the branches of the rock elm, even if she could hobble to the window.

At the foot of the Schoonover drive, Roland pulled me close.

Days of seeing him without touching him had made me crazy. His breathing was harsh and he kissed me hard, but then he pushed me away. "She'll be waiting. And somehow, she knows something. Maybe she doesn't know about you, but she knows *something*." Resting his forehead on my shoulder, he groaned, "What's to be done?"

"You keep asking that. I don't think there's *anything* to be done."

I wanted to toss away any restraint I owned—not much, God knows—and thrust myself against him.

He held my arms now, keeping me inches away. "*Whatever* it was she thought," he said, "she'd take it out on *you*." He kissed me lightly and stepped back. "I'll watch till you're at the gate. Give 'em my best."

Approaching the gate, I smelled tobacco. Alone in the deepening twilight, sitting on the back steps, Dennis said, "Lover boy walk you home?"

I started. He couldn't have seen Roland kiss me; the lilac bushes along the dooryard fence stood in the way.

"Please don't," I said, my skirt brushing his arm as I passed into the house. I hated that I was trembling and sounded small and unsure.

In the kitchen, I told Emma, "Roland walked me to our drive. He says there's a wild dog wandering around, and that we should keep the back gate closed so Teddy can't get out."

She nodded. "I heard it last night. It'll be after the chickens too. I shut the hen house door. They oughta do the same." She ladled a cup of water from the bucket beside the sink. "You must be tired. Go up to bed." I *was* tired and I did go up.

Although both my windows were open, no breeze from the east or south wandered the yard looking for me. I stood peering across the road. The night was breathless hot and so quiet you could hear crops growing. Out in the dark, night creatures moved about—raccoons and owls, field mice and prowling barn cats—each on his own mission. And somewhere, maybe close, there was a feral dog. Would he or she tempt another dog to come away on a wild roam? Was that what the howling was about? A plea? An invitation? I couldn't help sympathizing with the orphaned creature. Still, I wouldn't want to meet it in the dark.

Before I extinguished the lamp, I heard the howl, a bone-chilling ululation. The dog was on the road somewhere between our farm and the two cemeteries.

Now Teddy, chained by the back door, answered, his howl as ringing and plaintive as the other. Then Red, locked in the barn across the road, joined them, muffled but lamenting. The sound was nothing I wanted to hear again, a chorus of anguished yearning.

I fell asleep listening.

"Get out!"

In the doorway, I jumped, startled by Dora pitching the jar of wilted daisies across the room. "You think I don't know that you're judging me every time you come through that door? I can feel it." Her chin jutted. "And who are you to judge? What do *you* know? How to be a farmhand? How far will that take you?"

Things had been testy between us, but throwing things was childish, even for Dora. Still, I had to consider what might have happened between Roland and Dora overnight, what might have hurt and upset her.

I knelt beside the door, picking up the daisies and the unbroken jar. "I'll get a cloth to wipe this up," I said and left.

Yesterday, she'd pitched a fit at being asked to use the commode instead of the bedpan. I told her she ought to go on the stage; she'd give Sarah Bernhardt a run for her money. She was now perfectly able to heave herself out of bed and onto the commode, but seemed to derive a peculiar pleasure from making me help her with the bedpan, though, really, the bedpan couldn't have been a picnic.

The truth was, with help, she was strong enough to maneuver herself down the stairs, where she could sit on the sofa and read a book. Or I'd have read to her, if she'd let me. She was growing too accustomed to the role of invalid.

Add to this, she'd developed a deep dislike for me. Female instinct, perhaps. Everything I did annoyed her, especially the things I did *for* her. Still, she wouldn't do them for herself.

Back in her room, on my hands and knees, wiping up the water, I asked, "What do you want for lunch?" She didn't reply. In the few minutes that I was downstairs fetching a rag, she'd wound herself into a tighter coil of anger. Rising, I wiped the perspiration from my face with the hem of my apron. "Cold chicken and iced tea? Maybe some braised onions and a slice of bread and butter?"

She glared at me. "Do you have any idea how much I dislike you?"

Try to keep her calm, I told myself. "I expect I do, but why is it that you dislike me?"

"You're smug and uppity without reason. My husband thinks you're feebleminded."

Lying about Roland, she'd pinched the wrong nerve. Tossing the rag aside, I crossed to the foot of her bed. In a subdued voice, I asked, "Do you suppose that saying 'my husband' makes you a wife? You're no wife, Dora. You're a . . . a slug, like the ones that eat the cabbages in the garden.

"Maybe you married Roland because you thought you'd make a handsome couple? But last time I heard, the saying was still 'pretty is as pretty does.' At that rate, another year and you'll be as ugly as a warthog, because you do nothing." I headed for the door. "I'll be watering the garden. If you have to pee, you can get yourself to the commode." Turning back, I asked, "What did you imagine farm life was?"

Taking me by surprise, she began to weep. "Maybe it's true that I don't do anything," she whimpered, "but nothing was like I imagined. I never even visited a farm before Roland married me. I sure never imagined it'd be like *this*. Manure and dust and flies and awful smells. And work and work and work! Roland's never had time to teach me anything."

She threw herself back against the pillows. "Mrs. Know-it-all across the road tried, but she took a dislike to me."

"Dora, Emma does know it all. For someone so ignorant, you're awfully arrogant."

"And you're a monster," she mewled. "Did you come here to make me crazy, so Roland could put me in that place with the other crazy people?" She kicked at the sheet. "You've never been married. No, and you've never had a baby. I had one, and she died." God knew that was true.

She wept, the uncontrolled weeping of a child. And, like a child's weeping, it fed upon itself till she was flinging herself around. "You're like that one across the road. Why are you so mean?"

"I'm not mean, and neither is Emma. But you were the 'beautiful princess' for too many years. Out *here* in the country, people will treat you the way you deserve, not the way you *look*. Anyway, you don't look beautiful right now. Your face is all red and screwed up like a monkey's."

What I'd said frightened her. "I was the prettiest girl in Harvester. Ask anybody."

"And how far will that take you?" I asked, throwing her earlier words back at her.

How sad. If all you loved about yourself was your beauty, and you couldn't count on that forever . . . It didn't make me like Dora, but maybe I was beginning to understand her a little.

And how could I—how could anyone—not be moved by these tears? Troubled, I turned to leave, my emotions in a muddle, my thoughts tangled. I needed to kneel and work in the garden.

When I returned later, Dora kept her face averted and her mouth sealed. I set the tray beside her on the bed and removed the pot from the commode.

Still later, bringing up a basin of water and a rag so she could tidy herself, I set a brush beside the basin. On those occasions when I'd seen her hair hanging loose, I'd noted how it fell in thick cascades. She and Roland *were* a beautiful pair. How had I dared to insert myself here?

Days went by without a word passing between Dora and me. The wind from the west continued dry and hot. The leaves on the rock elm were crisping. Emma told me that the lake had receded and Henry feared for the corn, which was burning up.

I prayed to all my gods and goddesses to make this summer disappear, like the thin dew in the hot morning. The grass in the yard was yellow, and I carried water to the garden twice a day, hoping Roland's well was deep.

I was certain that the quietly yet intensely Christian Moses knew about Roland and me, saw the looks that passed between us. Yet here, on the Allen farm, Roland and I were as chaste as little children. We could have found rare opportunities to meet behind the barn—where young boys, it is said, smoke their first corn silk. Beneath a scraggly Russian olive tree, beside a broken and rusted harrow, we could have torn at each other's clothing. I thought of it often, and sometimes pounded the kitchen table till my fists ached.

Each day, I crossed Cemetery Road at least once, seeking

Emma's advice about biscuits or dumplings, aphids or wasps' nests. And she might cross over to me with a hambone for bean soup or a cup of sweet-vinegar dressing for coleslaw.

Threshing season was ahead. "We'll have Roland's threshers at our house for meals," Emma said. "You can't handle all of it."

"Maybe Dora will take hold by then," I said.

"Don't hold your breath."

For days, neither Dora nor I uttered an extra syllable. Then one day I asked, "Do you love your husband?" The question had been plaguing me.

Dora was caught off guard. "What business is that of yours?" Though the room was airless and hot, she tucked the sheet tight around her, a defense against any assault I might be launching.

"In other words, you don't."

"Why do you say that?"

"If you loved him, you'd answer 'yes' without hesitating."

"You're wrong," she said without rancor.

I waited. "Some days I love him too much," she began, feeling her way. "And some days I hate him too much."

"Why do you hate him?"

She hesitated. Finally: "He has a . . . what you'd call a 'mistress.'" For Dora, "mistress" was high-flown. She spoke the word as though it were from the French.

"A mistress?" I asked in an unbelieving voice, smiling as if she'd said something quite unlikely. Cold sweat collected beneath my arms.

"I have proof," she said with satisfaction, and pulled herself to the side of the bed. I waited, rigid with apprehension.

From beneath a linen scarf on the bedside table, she extracted a piece of paper, much the worse for its many foldings and refoldings. The note I had slipped to Roland on the Fourth of July.

*My God.* If I'd been able to move, I'd have sprinted down the stairs and across the fields.

Dora's mouth pulled up in a sly half smile. I forced the words. "What's that?"

"It's for me to know and you to guess." What game was this? But she continued, "Her name starts with a *B.*"

*What?*

"You see?" She held the note out to me. I didn't take it; my unsteady hand would have betrayed me. But I could see that the *R* for Ruby had bled, perhaps from Roland's perspiration that hot day. Now the letter did resemble a *B.* The rest was blurry but could be read. *Darling Roland, I love you with all my heart. I long to touch you. Yours,*

"Barbara?" Dora asked. "Bernice? Betty? Some town girl."

I shrugged. "I don't know anyone in town, except store people," I told her.

Dora dug beneath her pillow for a handkerchief. "So I know Roland's got a mistress." She mopped her tears.

What held me there? Pity? Paralyzing relief? At length, I sat down on the bed and took one of Dora's hands, patting it. "How did you come by this note?"

"It fell out of Roland's overalls when he took them off. After that picnic on Fourth of July. Somehow it got swept under the bed. I saw him looking for it and trying not to let me see, so I knew it must be important.

"I was suspicious already, so when he left the room, I found it. It nearly killed me."

*Indeed. But for Moses.*

# CHAPTER FOURTEEN

I had never dreamed that Dora might love Roland. I still wasn't certain that she did.

A couple of days later, I asked her, "If you could change your life, how would you change it?" Why did I ask? I didn't really want to know.

"If I could change my life," Dora said, "there wouldn't be any Barbara or Bernice, or whoever she is."

"But there is a Barbara or Bernice or somebody," I said.

She anguished, "Do you have to say that? It hurts . . . like a knife. You don't know how bad it hurts." Her face twisted with pain, pain that I could understand. Pain that *I* would feel if Roland loved someone else.

I cast about for a metaphor. "When the doctor set your bones, it must have hurt. But he had to do it so they could heal."

With annoying literalness, she pointed out, "But he gave me something. Ether or chloroform, so I didn't feel it."

"Well, just imagine how bad it would have hurt if he hadn't given you that, and setting the bones was still necessary in order for them to heal. Can you imagine that?"

She nodded, though she was obviously uncertain about this metaphor.

"It's the same with imagining Barbara. First you have to accept that she exists. You have to feel the pain of knowing that before you can do anything."

"Do anything, like what?"

She had no idea what our conversation was costing me. And I had no idea why I was exploring this with her. I must be demented.

"For heaven's sake, Dora, I don't know what! What would make Roland happy?" I knew some things that would make him happy, but I wasn't going to point them out. I wasn't *that* demented. "Do you want him back?" She nodded. Each word I uttered wizened some happy place in me.

"You think about it, Dora. Think about what Roland would like." I picked up the breakfast tray and started for the door. "I have to get to work now."

"What will you be doing?"

"Washing dishes, gathering eggs, feeding the chickens, watering the garden, starting the next meal, baking a cake. The same things I generally do."

"In this heat?"

"In this heat."


I headed downstairs, wondering if I was helping Dora to win Roland back. If so, I might just as well throw my own noose over a barn beam. I did the things that I'd told Dora I would do. I did them blindly and without thought, all the time imagining losing Roland. Then I sat crumpled at the table.

After long minutes, I rose and went through the motions of getting the midday meal on the table. As the two men ate, I was silent. Roland looked questions at me. I picked at the chicken and potatoes on my plate.

The afternoon of the following day, Dora said, "I've been thinking."

"About what?"

"Whether I want to get Roland back."

"Why wouldn't you want to?"

"I'm angry, and I hate him most of the time. Think about it, Ruby. Think about what he's done, how he's made me look to the town, to my family."

Unlike jealousy or sorrow or hatred, which had the possibility of being hidden from sight, humiliation was public. It paraded your failures on Main Street. And it led to hatred, even of the one you loved most, especially of the one you loved most.

I understood that. But I didn't understand myself or what was going on between Dora and me. I tried to view myself as if from a great distance, but when you are young, perspective is next to impossible. So Dora and I would have to muddle along as we were, each of us groping our way, each of us praying for a different outcome.

"The first thing you have to decide," I told Dora, "is: Do you want to be married to Roland?"

"Do I have a choice?"

I thought about that. Divorce was a terrible scandal in Harvester, worse by far than trying to kill yourself. Was Dora the sort of person who could endure that? If not, and she moved, how on earth would she support herself? She had no skills.

"*Well?*" she pressed. "Do I have a choice?"

How to tell her that she was hopeless? "What can you do?" She was perplexed. "Can you bake a cake or milk a cow or plant a garden? What can you do?" I repeated.

Her face grew serious. She was scratching the hard earth of her ignorance, hoping to find some seed of promise.

Between us, we found that she could cook "a little" and do some laundry, though she hated it, especially in winter. "My hands get so red and cracked," she said.

"My God," I sighed, "you've only got one talent, and that's a pretty face, and that's no talent at all."

Her features clouded over. She was going to bawl again.

"Think!" I said before her lip started quivering.

"I am thinking!"

"If something happened to Roland, what could you do to earn your keep?"

"Nothing's going to happen to him." She sniffled, reaching for her handkerchief.

"Have you ever noticed how hard he works? And only Moses to help him? Roland's killing himself, you . . ." I left her to mull this over. She was not a quick study, and my head was reeling. Well, not exactly reeling—more like grinding round and round, an eddy of gravel and muck. Nothing was clear.

The evening was going lavender when I crossed Cemetery Road. Despite the dry weather, frogs croaked in the ditch, and in the trees cicadas whined.

Since we hadn't heard the wild dog the past two nights, I told Roland not to accompany me. Dora would soon be getting around and keeping an eye on him. We had to be discreet.

Dennis was sitting on the back steps again, smoking, with Teddy at his feet. The smell of cigarette smoke was heavy and pleasant in the still-hot evening air. I liked the scent and thought that I wouldn't mind learning to smoke. Maybe I should ask Dennis to teach me before he left for college. A woman who smoked in public was considered "loose," but I saw no harm in smoking if it was in private. And in any case, why was it immoral only for a woman and not a man?

"I like the smell of your cigarettes," I said as I turned in at the gate. "Would you teach me how to smoke?"

"You don't want to do that. You're a nice girl. You *are* a nice girl, aren't you?"

"Yes." I sat down beside him. Was I a nice girl?

"Well, then, you don't want to smoke."

"That makes no sense. If I like the smell, I don't see why I shouldn't smoke. I won't do it on Main Street—just out here on the steps in the evening. You'll be leaving for college pretty soon, and then whose cigarettes will I smell?"

"Jake and Henry smoke pipes."

"That's not the same. Please teach me. I won't tell anyone. It'll be our secret." I could see that he liked the idea of us having a secret.

Before passing me his cigarette, he said, "The important thing when you're learning is not to choke on the smoke. You'll have a coughing fit if you do. Just suck the smoke into your mouth quick and blow it out again, until you get the hang of it."

I drew in smoke the way he suggested, blowing it out again immediately. It seemed awfully simple, innocent, and frankly silly. There must be more to it than this.

"Eventually you'll learn to inhale," he said. He took the cigarette back again, illustrating the technique. Inhaling was not so simple. I tried it and, as he'd warned, choked and coughed. Still, I was thrilled to have tried, and I knew I'd acquire the knack.

"If I give you money, will you buy me some tobacco and papers Saturday, when you're in town?"

With Christian reluctance but wanting to please me, he agreed and we shook hands on it. "Thank you," I said, "you are a good friend."

I gave his shoulder a sisterly squeeze and opened the screen door.

. . .

"You've lost weight." Emma studied me as I dipped water from the bucket. "That job across the road is too much. I should never have sent you over there."

"No, I'm making progress," I told her. Seeing Roland every day was worth any price. "Dora and I are talking. I think I can teach her things she needs to know, about being a farmwife."

Emma shook her head. "And what are you getting out of this teaching and all the hard work that goes with it?" She poured me a cup of reheated coffee and lay several cookies beside it on the table.

She was concerned for me, but I knew she was also concerned for Roland. This was not an easy summer for Emma. Ignoring her question, I asked after Henry.

"Gone to bed with the birds." Thoughtful, she sat down at the table, folding her hands in front of her. "In the beginning, with Roland being hard up, I thought it'd be the right thing, your goin' across the road. It'd save him money and you'd be good company for both of 'em. But I don't like you losing weight this way. When I get you back here again, I'll fatten you up," she said. "Now, off to bed with you."


As soon as the sky was black, the wild dog began howling, the sound coming from the direction of the lake this time. Maybe he'd gone for a swim.

I wished that we could adopt him, but he'd probably grown too wild for that. Whenever I heard his crying, I remembered Roland saying, "He's lost his people." Before extinguishing the lamp, I wrote a quick note to Professor Cromwell, trying to describe the sound of the dog and how it made me feel.

"It has a hold on me, right down in my soul. The dog has

been doing damage, ravaging animals—ducks and chickens and even small dogs—on the farms around here, but if someone kills him, and they *will*, the gods won't be happy. That's what I feel."

When I brought up Dora's breakfast tray the following morning, she waylaid me.

"I've been thinking." She plucked at the sheet.

"What, again?" Setting the tray on the bed, I waited. I was always waiting for her to say something intelligent.

"I've been doing what you told me, thinking about what if something happened to Roland." She paused. "I need to learn how to do things."

"Yes."

"What things?"

"How to cook? And bake, maybe?"

Her mouth turned downward at the thought.

"Would you rather start with laundry?"

"Isn't there something pleasant?"

The timing of our plans was uncanny. The next day the doctor removed Dora's casts. She was not altogether pleased by this new, if partial, freedom. I say "partial" because Dora had not been following the doctor's order to exercise. Freedom was not what she longed for, I could see. A cage was what she longed for, like a pretty bird.

I had thought that she'd be eager to lose the casts. Now she could get to the window and even downstairs to check on Roland. But apparently she was torn between that and her reluctance to work. She was lazy and silly and childlike. Childlike must have been her appeal when Roland married her.

After I'd seen the doctor to his buggy, I climbed the stairs. "Now what?" I asked Dora. "Are you going to lie around or are you going to learn something? Make up your mind. Emma can't do without me forever."

. . .

Emma was crimping the crust of an apple pie before sliding it
into the oven. In hot weather, she baked at night.

"Dora got the casts off today," I told her.

She wiped floury hands on her apron, then mopped her face
with a rag and sat down, heaving with exhaustion. "She'll be
weak as a kitten for some time. Roland'll still need you. I miss
you, but we'll make do here a while longer."

"I feel like I'm losing touch with you folks."

"Don't worry, little girl, you're still my right hand."

"When does Dennis leave?"

"Two-three weeks. We'll have a little party before he goes.
Us and them across the road."


In bed, I tried to reach out to Serena, wherever she was. Some
nights I talked to her and felt her listening. Tonight, I wanted to
tell her about my conversations with Dora. But she wasn't close.
She came and went.

Toward morning, I dreamed I was climbing the roof of
Roland's barn and lost my grip at the top, falling, screaming. I
landed on the floor beside my bed, and Dennis was there helping
me back into bed and telling me it was just a dream.

But I was shaken and shivering despite the suffocating heat
in the room. The sky in the east was pink and yellow and pearly.
Four-thirty. I dressed and went down to the kitchen, thinking
how kind Dennis had been. I hoped his father wouldn't make
him go into the newspaper business.

In the dim kitchen, I sat at the table, my mind back in the
dusty farmyard on which I'd lain broken. As the sun tipped over
the horizon, I saw two apple pies on the table, and also cookies
piled on a platter. The amazing Emma.

I walked out to the yard and crossed to the barn, stumbling as I glanced up at its steep roof. Grabbing a stool from where it hung, I began milking the cows. The barn cats, hearing the ping of milk in the pail, came running.

This was a satisfying time of day, a satisfying occupation. Alone with the cats and cows, and while the others were dressing or coaxing the big stove to life, I could dream my waking dreams uninterrupted.

When I had finished, I opened the door to the pasture, backed the cows from their stanchions, and urged them out. It required little urging as they were eager to wend their unhurried way down to the cool, shady end.

Now I carried water to the garden, checking for slugs and aphids and beetles and mold. Second and even third crops of some vegetables renewed the need for vigilance. If I found a dying tomato plant, one that had been staunch and healthy the previous day, it was cause for tears. We, Emma and I, had sown the seeds, hauled old manure, nurtured and watered and tended, so where precisely did the blame lie when a plant folded upon itself? The death always felt personal and left me feeling guilty.

Moving on, I gathered eggs from beneath indignant hens, affronted biddies, loath to give up their intimate produce. When I left, they nattered among themselves, disgruntled.

In the kitchen, Emma nodded toward the table. "There's cookies to go. Roland does like them oatmeal ones with the black walnuts."

I set the egg basket on the counter. "I'd best get across the road," I said. "It's getting late." But the straightforward peace of this place had a grip on me, and I had to force myself away.

# CHAPTER FIFTEEN

After helping Dora to use the commode, I found clean undergarments and a cotton dress, draping them over the foot of the bed while I straightened the sheets and plumped the pillows.

We brushed her hair, sponged her face and arms, and began the long, arduous descent of the stairs, resting at every third step. Too long out of commission, her limbs were weak and unreliable.

She wanted to sit in the sun, she said, so I carried a kitchen chair into the dusty, wind-seared yard, settling her near the garden to observe while I watered, telling her, "You'll be doing this, so watch how many pails I carry." Looking vexed, she twisted her hands in her lap.

"The day after a good rain, Dora, don't water. If you do, the vegetables will get mold and the roots will rot." I added, "Right now, everything's scorched. I only hope the well doesn't give out."

"Could it do that?"

"It could, but I'm thinking that any week now we're due for a drencher." No point in worrying her unduly. She could handle only so many challenges at a time.

Dora's gaze followed me as I plucked dried leaves from a second crop of peas and pulled up weeds from beneath tomato plants. After several minutes, she asked, "What do you think, Ruby? Is Roland still seeing that woman?"

"When would he find the time?"

"When he goes to town?"

We'd braided her hair into a long plait down her back. She reached for it now, as if to examine it. Turning it this way and that, her face thoughtful, she said, "In my mind, I call her Barbara. I can almost see her. I think she's different from me. I think she's dark and pretty, like you. And I think she gardens."

"You think too much." My voice was steady, but an artery in my neck was thumping as I passed her, returning to the trough beneath the windmill. When I'd emptied that pailful, I told her, "If you went to town with him, you'd put an end to any visits from a girlfriend—if there is one."

"I couldn't go to town."

"Why not?"

"People know that I'm disowned. And by now, they surely know about the other," she said, tilting her head toward the barn. "I couldn't face 'em." She shook her head and flung the plait over her shoulder. "I don't want to talk about it."

I hoed between rows of vegetables, loosening the dirt, checking the depth of my watering, then went back to the trough.

"Are you going to remember what I'm doing here?" I asked, drawing her attention back to the garden. I dumped water around the base of the bean vines, then straightened, telling her, "When I'm done, we'll walk up to the gate and back. You can use the cane Emma sent over."

This tutorial journey of Dora's and mine took us down a rough road. She was as stubborn and doubtful as an untrained mule. Though she was lazy witted, she was not entirely stupid, and she had a streak of canniness that responded to "What if something happened to Roland?" She did not want to end up living on the County Poor Farm.

That first week out of the casts, Dora merely sat and watched me work, though I insisted that she practice with the cane, moving from room to room, from indoors to outdoors, and, finally, from upstairs to downstairs and back. She used the commode at night, the outhouse during the day. The trip to the outhouse—down the back steps, around the side of the house, up one step into the building, then turning and lowering herself—all this was excellent exercise.

But she fretted over her limp. "It just wears me out, Ruby, and I ache all over." I knew that was true. "And I look like an old hag."

More than once, she burst into tears. "It's not getting any better, Ruby! Will I always limp?"

Even I was moved. "It'll get better if you keep exercising. And before long your leg will be so strong, you probably won't have a limp at all." Vanity was a better prod than a sharp stick.

Finally determined to recapture Roland, Dora now came to the table at meals, even breakfast, and expressed great care for her husband. Handing him a handkerchief when he sneezed, she said, "The haying dust must be awful. I'll keep a supply of clean handkerchiefs ready."

Two days earlier, we had done laundry, including handkerchiefs. Rather, I had done the laundry, and Dora had observed. As I was feeding the last load into the wringer, she rose from her chair, insisting, "I can do that," and hitching herself across the porch with the cane.

Moving to the side, I passed her one item at a time and she fed each into the rollers as I cranked. We were nearly done when I folded a final shirt to make certain it fit the width of the wringer.

If an article was too wide, it jammed the mechanism and would end up torn or stained with machine oil.

Handing her the shirt, I said, "This is the last. Keep it folded."

One moment she was feeding the cloth in, and the next she was yowling. I grabbed the release knob on the wringer, and the rollers sprang apart. Tearful and frightened, she turned, holding out her hand.

"Can you make a fist?" I asked.

Trembling, she curled the fingers.

"It'll bruise, but nothing's broken."


Opening the screen door at the Allens' one morning, I smelled meat frying. Dora stood at the stove turning pieces of steak in a skillet. In a second pan, she'd scrambled eggs. On the table, a stack of toast—some charred but toasted nonetheless—sat on a chipped plate, a jar of Emma's apple butter alongside.

Dora turned, smiling. "See what I've done, Ruby? Aren't you proud of me?" She forked steak onto a platter. "I gathered eggs. The hens pecked me, but I gave them what for." She giggled. Again she asked, "Aren't you proud of me?"

Some part of me that was bold and sure and strong was fraying along the edges. What had I done?

We crammed the next three weeks with lessons. She still used the cane and she still limped, but she was moving with fewer mishaps and could even lower herself onto a milking stool. "That shows courage," I told her. Well, it did.

The last and most reluctant of Dora's assignments had been learning to milk. She was frightened of the cows and they knew it, rolling their eyes and shifting their hooves. Milking required several sessions, the two of us together.

For her solo performance, I left her alone. Afterward, she was querulous and shaken. "How do I get them to stand still?"

"If they kick, you'll have to hobble them. But once they're used to you and they know you're competent, they'll quiet down. Pat them and talk to them. They've got names. Right now, they know you're nervous, and that makes *them* nervous."

At the end of the day, when I climbed the stairs to the bedroom under the eaves, my shoulders sagged. In front of Emma or Dora, I held them straight. I was a strong girl. A plucky girl. Emma was proud of me. Dora admired my grit. But when I was alone, I knew that I was weak and confused. Confused about Dora and Roland and me.

One morning, while Dora gathered eggs, Roland told me, "I want to be a good farmer, Ruby. Like Henry. I want to study it." Moses nodded, pouring syrup over his pancakes. "Henry told me there're books in the St. Bridget library about what crops to plant for maximum yield and how to rotate them to get the best use of the land," Roland went on. "I've got a library card. When threshing's done, I'm gonna check out some of those books."

Surely I was meant to be part of that, to read the books, work hard all day, and, when night came, go to bed with Roland. We were two lines of a rhymed couplet.

Sighing over all this, one night I lay down on my bed and reached for Whitman. But lying on top of that was a letter from Professor Cromwell.

"I loved your last letter," he wrote. "When you describe the work on the farm and the things you love about the place, I can almost see them. I, too, am fond of cottonwoods, despite the 'cotton' that clogs the screen door. The lush, pendulous limbs and the shining leaves that turn up their undersides to announce coming rain, these are indeed worthy of our praise and affection. You say that cottonwoods want to please, that they will grow with their roots in the water at the lake's edge, or with their roots in the hot, dry soil of the season you're currently experiencing. Do not blush, little Ruby, when I say that their adaptability reminds me of you.

"On the topic of adaptability, you and Dora seem to be growing used to each other as the weeks pass. Maybe this is proof against the notion that the leopard can't change his spots. Or maybe she's simply seen the practicality of doing the right thing. I do believe that if one does the right thing long enough, the behavior becomes ingrained and irreversible.

"I wonder if bachelorhood has become ingrained in me and irreversible. Between my teaching and the laboratory work, I have few hours left for socializing, but I like to think I wouldn't be averse if the opportunity arose."

I rather doubted that he had no opportunities for socializing. He was, as I recalled, a handsome man and one with prospects.

"And speaking of socializing," he continued, "I recently paid a call on your great-aunt, who is now confined to her bed and extremely frail. Still, she did appreciate the visit and asked if I would read to her from the Bible, since the book is too heavy for her to lift. She requested something from the New Testament, saying that the Old Testament was too dark for her present mood. I think she sees the end coming and finds the New Testament more reassuring.

"I am glad to hear that despite heavy work, you carve out time for books. Some people find Whitman shocking, but you have a sophisticated mind. His love of all things human, flesh and spirit, would appeal to you. It fits with your love of the earthiness of farming. Whitman finds the body and the soul to be one and the same. It is not Christian orthodoxy, but it is refreshing, and I'm not sure that I disagree."

He closed with, "Don't forget your Beardsley friends, among whom I count myself. We would welcome your return."

In reading each of Professor Cromwell's letters, I came away with a slightly altered view of myself. That is one of the gifts of a valued friendship. Extinguishing the lamp, I fell into a deep sleep.

The next morning, as I prepared to cross Cemetery Road, Emma asked, "Did you hear the wild dog last night? Sounded like he was in Roland's grove."

She reached into the icebox for the cream pitcher. Turning, she said, "The thing'd break your heart if he wasn't so dangerous."

# CHAPTER SIXTEEN

S aturday night after chores, Henry took the men, including Roland and Moses, to Reagan's for beer. "Next week
is threshing," Henry told them. "Let's have a good time
Saturday night."

When the kitchen table was cleared, the dishes washed, and
the men gone, Dora begged, "Stay till Roland and Moses come
back? I get scared when they're gone."

We sat on the back stoop in the fading light, surrounded by
the restlessness of trees and the chirruping of crickets. Curious
about something I had never known, I asked Dora about high
school.

"I had a lot of friends," she said, recalling days of lightness and
ease, girlfriends and beaux. "I suppose it was because I was pretty.
When I was a senior, I was Queen of the May, and I wore a long
white dress and a crown of flowers." The nostalgia in her voice was
artless, easily evoking lost dolls and hoops and hair ribbons.

"Would you be shocked if I smoked a cigarette?" I asked.

She looked at me, seeing me in some new way, her face pale
and lovely in the near dark. "No. I knew a girl in high school

whose brother let her smoke part of his cigarette when he rolled one." She went on, "I never could see the use of cigarettes, but I don't mind if you want to smoke."

We were quiet for long minutes, and when I had taken the first puff, she said, "I do kind of like the smell. How does it taste?"

"Like . . . adventure. Don't ask me what I mean by that, because I don't know."

She nodded. "That's how I felt about getting married. It was an adventure." She shifted, tucking her skirt close around her. "I thought I'd be my own boss."

"Is anyone ever their own boss?"

"Not on a farm, apparently; the weather's the boss. Locusts are the boss. Death is the boss."

From the barn, where Roland had locked him, Red whined with deep grievance and heartache.

"Should we let him out?" Dora asked.

"Roland's afraid he'll run off with the wild dog."

"But he sounds sick with unhappiness. Maybe he *wants* to be wild."

"He's a domesticated animal. He might die living wild."

"Oh, look," Dora exclaimed, lifting a hand. Around us, fireflies flickered and danced, incandescent souls trapped between earth and heaven. "Did you ever catch them in a jar?" she asked.

"Serena and I, we did that."

"Your mother."

"Sometimes she was like a little girl. We were growing up together. Did I ever tell you about the china tea set and the gazebo?" She shook her head. And so I told her, concluding, "I have the tea set but I'm still short a gazebo."

"It's sad," she said. "We both lost our mothers."

It had grown dark. I lit a second cigarette; the smoke seemed to keep the mosquitos away. We talked for another hour, then I asked, "What did you name your baby?"

"Lily."

"Lily Allen. With a name like that, I bet she'd grow up to be someone famous." Dora raised the hem of her apron and dabbed her eyes. "I didn't mean to hurt you," I said.

"It's all right. I like talking about her. Roland doesn't. But I think if you talk about somebody, it means they really existed. She only lived a few months, so sometimes it seems like I dreamed her."

"She existed. I saw her cradle. Do you have a photograph?"

"No. I wanted one after she died. They do that, you know, take pictures of people after they die, especially babies, so you have something to remember them by."

"But?"

"Roland didn't want to do that. He said it was morbid. It seemed like he hoped to forget the whole thing. I kind of understood, but I'd still have liked a picture."

"Did you bury her here on the farm?"

"She's in the Protestant cemetery down the road. Once in a while, I go there by myself. I want her to know I tried. And I loved her."

"You did your best."

"That's what worries me. My best wasn't good enough. She was small when she was born, and . . . and she did sort of go downhill. If I'd been smarter . . ." She shook her apron skirt in a gesture of frustration. "I'm stupid."

"You're not stupid. You just don't know very much. There's a difference. But look at what you've learned this summer. And learning tends to lead to more learning."

She appeared heartened by this. "Is there any coffee left?" she wondered, rising.

Later, we sat at the table drinking warmed-up coffee and eating cookies. Around ten-thirty we decided to play checkers, but then Red set up a howl inside the barn, throwing himself against the door.

I snatched the lantern from the table and ran to the porch, grabbing the broken spade handle. As I hurtled out and down the steps, a hen in the center of the farmyard squawked and thrashed and fluttered in the brainless way hens do when upset. Why was it there? A gibbous moon shone enough light to reveal the henhouse door standing open.

I waited, listening, but the only sounds were the chicken and, inside the barn, Red howling and banging. Raising the lantern and carrying the spade handle, I started toward the henhouse, glancing around as I went.

Then, from the shadows beside the barn, a large black dog slunk out, crouching and, with infinite care, laying down one paw at a time on the hard, dry earth. It froze for an endless moment before streaking silent across the yard, leaping in an arc and pouncing on the confused chicken as the bird ran in circles. Clutching the fowl in its jaws, the dog gave it one violent shake, and the squawking ceased.

Now I was racing, wielding the cudgel in a circle above my head. The dog dropped the chicken and stood facing me, teeth bared, guttural rumbling warning me not to come closer. But I had blood in my eye. Dropping the lantern, I held the stick with both hands, like a bat. Swinging it in front of me, I shot forward.

The vaulting dog and I met with a deathly crack across the side of his head. He fell at my feet. I stood swaying. What had happened? I moved closer. He didn't stir. His lips were still drawn back in a snarl. Then his body convulsed, his spine seizing in a spasm. I screamed.

Dora came running. "Ruby! Ruby!" She stopped, staring at the dog, then: "Are you all right?" She held me. "You ran out so fast, I didn't know what was happening. Are you all right?" she asked again.

Weak and shaking, I let her lead me back to the house,

gathering up the lantern on the way. "What have I done?" I asked. "What have I done?"

Dora made me tea from the last in the tin. But when I'd sipped some of it, I laid my head on the table. Near midnight, we heard Henry's automobile snorting down the road, letting Roland and Moses out at the gate. Dora ran to meet them.

As they opened the screen door, she was telling them, "And it's still out in the yard, the dead hen too. You should walk her home, Roland. She's weary to death."

"What have I done, Roland?" I asked. "I killed a poor hungry thing. I lost my senses."

"Hush." He helped me up, supporting me as I stumbled toward the door.

"He was an orphan, Roland, and . . . and he was only doing what any hungry creature would do. An orphan."

A cloud bank covered the gibbous moon as Roland guided me across an inky Cemetery Road and up the long Schoonover drive.

In the vast darkness around us, no dogs howled.


I lay awake for hours, tossing. Somewhere in the night, I pleaded with Serena, "Tell me what happened. What have I done? Why do I feel this dark, terrible loss?"

# CHAPTER SEVENTEEN

H ot weather continued through threshing. As she'd promised, Emma fed the threshers in the Schoonover kitchen. Avoiding the heat of the day, at night Dora and I turned out cakes and pies to contribute. And digging up early season potatoes from the Allen garden, we tossed together great batches of German potato salad. Roland's sweet corn had weathered the heat better than Henry's, so we cleaned dozens of ears to boil and carry.

Although Dora's pies were slipshod looking and their crusts somewhat tough, they were toothsome and that was all the threshers demanded. And it did not go amiss that the baker was young and pretty. For those two weeks in the Schoonover kitchen, we women were coquettish and silly, even Emma. Dora flirted with each of the men, without favor, Roland included. Possibly to annoy "lover boy," shy Dennis was lavish in his praise of Dora's cookery.

For the first time since I'd known her, Dora relaxed, moving with the tempo of feverish days, taking the lack of sleep in stride. Despite a continuing limp, she'd managed to abandon the cane.

At night, after the visiting threshers had left and before
each of us began preparing food for the next day, Emma, Dora,
and I stole half an hour to sit on the Schoonover front porch on
chairs dragged out from the kitchen. Fanning ourselves with
paper fans from Redene's Funeral Parlor—"Let Us Prepare
Your Loved One for His Heavenly Welcome"—we spoke in
muted voices. In the scruffy grass, crickets sang a homely song,
and I recalled summer nights in childhood when crickets were
friends who sang me to sleep. Half a mile down Cemetery Road,
on Sioux Woman Lake, a loon launched its inconsolable cry. I
paused at the sound.

On these nights, hot and sultry, I smoked cigarettes. At first
Emma made a small offended sound, but then she shrugged and
said nothing. Occasionally, Dora took a drag. Several evenings,
Emma poured a tot of something bold for each of us, a liquor she
used in her mincemeat recipe, "like my ma."

The last night of threshers working at the Schoonovers',
Emma handed Dora and me each a shot to revive us, saying,
"The both of you has lost a good five pounds, and you'd neither
of you five to lose." Lifting her glass, she said, "Here's to hard-
workin' women." I could not imagine life being pleasanter than
this, unless I were alone with Roland—and in these febrile days,
we had no opportunity to speak except in front of others.

Climbing the stairs after midnight, I fell at once into a stu-
por of sleep. Strange to say, it wasn't Roland but the dog who
nightly visited my dreams, each time falling dead at my feet, each
time howling even as he lay lifeless, the same howling I had heard
those evenings as I stood at the window.

What had I done? I had killed a hungry creature, an orphan.
People, threshers included, kept congratulating me, telling me
the dog had been slaughtering chickens, domesticated rabbits,
and ducks. I ought to get a reward, they said. I'd done everyone
a favor.

. . .

The second week, when the threshers worked at the Allen farm, they continued eating their meals at the Schoonovers'. But Dora and I carried rest-break sandwiches and watermelon slices out to them in the field, along with cool water.

And we went on, as before, working into the night. On one such late night, we sat at the table playing two-handed patience while we waited for pies to bake.

Parceling out the deck of cards, three at a time, onto the pile in front of her, Dora said, "I never worked so hard. I never did much *work* at all—before I got married, anyway."

"Serena made me do a little work every day, when I was small," I said. "But she made it seem like play."

"I was a house pet," Dora explained, "like a cat or dog." She thought about that for a moment. Then, laying a queen of diamonds on a king of spades, she confessed, "When Emma said that about us being hardworking women, it made me feel good. Nobody ever said anything like that to me before."

"You can be proud."

"Did you know, Ruby, that if Roland had been a Baptist instead of a Methodist, my folks wouldn't have disowned me? They're powerfully strict Baptists. If they knew I'd smoked part of your cigarette or tasted Emma's liquor, I'd be double disowned."

Something about "double disowned" struck us as funny, and we laughed. "'Double-disowned Dora,'" I said. "It has a ring to it. Like 'Champagne Charlie.' We could write a song."

Looking suddenly unsure, Dora asked, "Do you think I'll go to hell for talking like this?"

"Girls are supposed to talk like this. Besides, if you go to hell, we'll pal around together."

. . .

The final Saturday of threshing, we were a group of twenty for Dennis's going-away-to-college party. Emma had invited the threshers and their wives. After finishing their work early, the visiting men headed home to wash up.

From Reagan's Saloon and Billiards in Harvester, Henry ordered a washtub of beer; Emma set out fried chicken, homemade rolls, a platter of sweet corn, a big bowl of sauerkraut, and a fancy dish of assorted pickles on her best cloth.

As Dora and I crossed Cemetery Road at six-thirty, carrying two cakes each, I pointed out the rising moon. Gigantic, the biggest I had ever seen, and orange, it loomed over Harvester, its face gazing down with a pensive, melancholy expression.

"Does it look sad to you?" I asked.

Dora studied it. "No. I think it looks jolly, like good things are coming."

Emma came to meet us when she heard the screen door. "Roland?"

"He'll be over in a few minutes, and Moses when he's finished milking."

"Did you see the harvest moon?" Emma asked.

"Ruby thinks it looks sad," Dora said. "I think it looks like good times. What do you think?"

Emma glanced at the moon, then at each of us. "Both, maybe."


After folks had eaten, I told an exhausted Emma to visit while Dora and I washed dishes. Some guests had spilled onto the front porch, carrying beer with them, while a number of men, Henry and Roland among them, sat down at the cleared kitchen table to play a version of poker requiring arguing, laughing, and hammering of fists. As Roland scooped in his cards, he glanced up, catching my eye and casting me a hungry look.

Three of the threshers' wives carried coffee cups into the parlor and settled into chairs more comfortable than they could afford at home. Pulling crochet-work from their bags, they bent their heads together to confer over some private matter and at length, determining guilt or innocence, they nodded knowingly and continued their handiwork.

Still later, I sat on the back steps with Dennis. In the hen-house close by, chickens in disturbed dreams clucked muffled displeasure.

"Are you excited?" I asked him.

"About what?"

"About college, of course."

He shrugged. "I guess. I don't expect I'll be there long. We'll be at war pretty soon. By Christmas, I think."

"Please don't say that."

"It'll happen. Wilson can't keep us out much longer."

We sat silent. Would Roland have to go if there was war?

"We're going to miss you. Come see us when you have a vacation."

"*You* won't miss me."

"Wrong. People can love each other without being romantic. I love Emma and Henry. And I love you."

"Not the way you love Roland."

"Oh, for pity's sake . . ."

"Sorry."

I reached into my apron pocket for cigarette makings. I rolled one for Dennis, another for myself. He lit them both.

"You taught me how to smoke," I reminded him.

"I'm sorry I did."

"Oh?"

"It's not ladylike."

"Ah, well, you don't think I'm a lady anyway."

"I never said that."

"Truth to tell, I'm not sure what a lady is."

The moon was high, no longer orange but so brilliant it cast shadows. The visiting horses nickered and moved restlessly, as if to say it was time to head home.

Exhaling smoke, Dennis asked, "Would you write me once in a while, you know, a line or so? Emma said she would."

"Of course. I like to write letters. It gives me a chance to see how I feel about things." I flicked ashes onto the brick walk. "I write something, I look at it, and I say, 'I had no idea that's what I thought.'"

Some minutes later, I ground out my cigarette and rose, tossing the stub under the porch. Bending, I kissed Dennis on the lips, then went inside.

The party was breaking up. Emma, Henry, and I trailed the guests to the back gate to see them off. Teddy appeared from somewhere, wagging his tail sociably. "Sorry I'm late," he seemed to say.

Last to leave were Dora, Roland, and Moses. When the good-nights were said, I watched them go down the drive, the still brilliant moon with its wide, pale aura picking out Dora's wifely arm tight around Roland's waist.

I knew the pain that came upon me was jealousy, but it felt like hate. I would not be able to endure it for long.

Beside me, Emma said, "You've done a good job."

# CHAPTER EIGHTEEN

Immediately following breakfast, Dennis's father was at the back door. They were journeying on to Minneapolis in Mr. Cansler's important-looking Ford sedan, loaded with boxes of whatever Dennis might need at the University of Minnesota, including the impressive new dictionary from Emma and Henry.

Henry, Emma, Jake, and I followed Dennis out the door, Emma pressing on him a packet of chicken sandwiches and cookies, Henry grabbing him by the shoulder and shaking his hand in a fashion both manly and fatherly. Having declined to come inside, an impatient Mr. Cansler stood on the brick walk twisting his hat in his hands.

Addressing Dennis's father, who seemed not of a sentimental turn, Henry said, "This is a fine, bright, hardworking boy you have, a young man anyone would be proud to call son. We will miss him."

Mr. Cansler nodded, thrust his hat on his head, pivoted, and was out the gate before we had time to send Dennis off properly. In this country, a proper send-off required no less than ten minutes of "Have you forgotten anything?" and "Write when you're settled" and "Sure I can't send some pie with you?"

All too quickly, Mr. Cansler was in the Model T, and Dennis was cranking the engine. Then they were clattering down the dusty drive and onto Cemetery Road, Emma and I waving them on their way.

Turning back to the house, I told Emma, "I'm staying home from church today. Correspondence. Do you mind?"

Something in my voice must have caught at her, for she hesitated, finally saying, "If you're staying home, would you run Dora's cake pans over to her?"

The things I had to do this day, I had to do alone and without conversation. Were I to speak of them, especially with Emma, I might well lose my nerve. I could so easily lose my nerve.

When Emma and Henry had left for church, I did indeed sit down at the kitchen table and dash off quick notes to Professor Cromwell and Mrs. Bullfinch. Too busy working with Dora, especially during the threshing weeks, I had been remiss. But now there were important requests I must make of my Beardsley friends, especially Professor Cromwell.

The envelopes sealed, stamped, and addressed, I grabbed the cake pans from the table and hurried out. At the Allens', the yard and house were quiet, the silence broken only by the crowing of a rooster, the clattering of the windmill, and, from the nearly dry creek in the pasture, the half-hearted maundering of one or two cows. Maybe the folks had all gone to church. For Dora, that would be a remarkable milestone.

Opening the screen door, I stepped into the porch. "Anybody home?" I called out, moving to the kitchen. No response. Laying the pans on the table, I wheeled, leaving again, pausing in the yard to check the garden.

It was dry, and vegetables remained to be harvested, so I began carrying pails of water. As I surveyed the tomatoes, arms crept around my waist.

"They're at church," Roland whispered. "Moses talked Dora into going with him."

Shucking our clothes, hands darting, we lay down on the dry, dusty grass beneath the rock elm, and I rained kisses on every inch of Roland I could reach, storing up memories of lips, eyelids, neck, arms, and legs.

After we had spent ourselves and lay in a swoon, I ran my hands over his shoulders and his clavicle, over the depression where clavicle met breastbone. I caressed his ribs and hip bones, the inside of his elbows, his belly, the trail of soft blond hairs leading to his groin. Finally, I kissed the calloused palms of his hands.

I ran my finger along the little half-moon scar beside his navel, where he told me he'd fallen on a piece of glass as a boy. On the inside of his thigh was a birth stain the size of a nickel and the color of a brown egg. His first two toes were identical in length, unlike mine, which descended like stair steps.

"I'll love you forever."

"Long as that?" he murmured.

"Yes, and if there's anything after that, I'll love you then too."

He told me that I was the wife of his soul, and I wept on his belly. In the tall grass by the road, mourning doves understood. Whitman's words scrolled across my brain. "To feed the remainder of life with one hour of fullness . . ."

Only when the sun was nearing eleven o'clock did we untangle ourselves, fearing Dora's sudden return. Then a reluctant unlacing of fingers, one final kiss, hasty dressing, Roland helping with my buttons. In moments I was headed back across the road, sobbing and shaking my clothes free of grass and dust.

After the midday meal and the washing up, I walked to town, memorizing the landscape as I went. My first stop was the

Milwaukee depot. From there, I headed to Main Street, dropping my letters into the outgoing slot in the post office lobby. There. It was done. Now I could tell Emma.

The street outside was ghostly, miniature cyclones of dust rising from the hard-packed earth as the wind blew down the bleached and empty corridor. From the post office, I trudged back into the country as the sun reached two-thirty in the sky. It threw a slanting light I have seen only on the prairie in late September and October, light with a tinge of amber and a tincture of despair. Given the smallest opportunity, it will sunder your heart.

When I had watered the garden and seen to it that plenty of corn was strewn about for the chickens, I went in search of Emma. Henry and Jake were sitting on the front porch smoking their pipes. Not finding her elsewhere, I went to Emma's bedroom door and called softly. Then I heard her stirring. "Yes?" She opened the door, straightening her skirt.

"Did I wake you?"

"No. It's time I was up." She led the way to the kitchen. "I wanta chip some ice off the block for a glass of cool water," she said, crossing to the icebox.

We sat at the table, fingering the sweat on the side of our glasses. "You wanted to say something," she ventured.

"I'm leaving," I told her. "Next Saturday, but please don't tell Roland or Dora."

She nodded. "I knew something was in the wind."

"You know I love you and Henry. It's nothing to do with you. You've been good to me, and I love the farm."

"It's Roland," she said.

I blinked.

"I knew from the start, something was gonna happen. Then, Fourth of July, it was there to be seen. I don't think you could help it." She held the glass against her forehead, rolling it back and forth. "You're the one I would have chosen for our Roland, but some things that are meant to be can never be. Maybe there's a lesson in that, but I don't know what it is."

The room under the eaves was stifling. I closed the door and stripped. Lying naked on the bed, I wept.

When I was done, I stood before the photograph of Serena and Denton. "I'm going back where I came from," I told them. "Being near you again is the only positive outcome of this journey. All the rest is pain."

Later, Emma came up to tell me I didn't have to come down to supper. She'd bring me something. A thousand fresh tears. She was my sister, my aunt, my cousin. She and Henry were my family. Around eight, she appeared with a plate of chicken, corn, and sliced tomatoes. She sat down at the side of the bed. "Do you have money?" she asked.

"I've saved most of my wages, and my friend Professor Cromwell sent money now and again, you remember."

"What will I do without you?"

"Don't worry. Plenty of girls would give their eyeteeth to work here."

She looked away and shook her head.

I lay staring at the ceiling, empty of thought, full of tears.

# CHAPTER NINETEEN

O n the farm, Emma kept silent about my leaving. But when we drove to town Monday morning, she spoke with two or three women and afterward placed an ad at the *Standard Ledger*. Between the conversations and the ad, she hoped to find my replacement.

"Won't Dora and Roland see the paper?" I didn't want Roland to know I was going until I'd left.

"I doubt they see it once a month."

Before returning to the farm, we stopped at the Harvester Arms Hotel and ordered coffee and doughnuts.

"I thought this place'd give us a chance to have a quiet chat, but now I can't think of anything to say," Emma told me. "I guess that's the way of things. You can't *plan* to talk; it has to come by itself."

"What I've been thinking," I said, "is Dora needs to learn how to can. They've still got vegetables in the garden, and so do we. Why don't we ask her to come over and learn?"

Emma nodded, taking a bite of doughnut and wiping crumbs from her lips. "We'll pick up jars while we're in town.

She likely hasn't any, except what we've brought over with some-thin' inside."

On the way home, Emma dropped me off at the Allens' driveway. "So you can see how she takes to the idea."

Dora was hauling water to the garden. In my chest, a small joy blossomed. The neophyte had begun taking hold of farm life. I grabbed another pail from the back porch and carried it to the trough.

At the kitchen table later, I watched Dora struggle with bread dough that wanted to stick to the board, despite its floured sur-face. Six weeks ago I would have taken a hand, but I'd seen that many things were best conquered alone.

"If you want to do this," I said, referring to the canning, "come over after breakfast tomorrow."

She nodded.

"Emma says we'll start with cucumbers. We've got a second crop and you do too. Bring your cukes and the jars you have."

A year from now, Dora might warm the breakfast coffee for me. If I were here. Right now, as Emma would say, showing the bread dough who was boss was all Dora could handle.

"Did I see you in the wagon with Moses yesterday, around noon?" I asked. I couldn't tell her that I had information of her churchgoing from Roland. "Looked like you were coming from town."

She paused in her kneading and, using the back of her hand, brushed her hair from her face. "I went to church with Moses."

"Good for you. Not that you went to church, but that you went to town. Was it scary?"

"It was sick-scary. In front of the Catholic church, I almost lost my breakfast. If my folks ever saw me going into a *Catholic* church . . ."

"They'd double-disown you."

She giggled. "Oh, worse than that. They'd probably shoot

me." The dough was coming together now, smooth and looking like something that might turn out to be bread.

I grabbed a bowl from the shelf, greased the inside with drippings, and handed it to her. She in turn greased the ball of bread dough and put it into the bowl. She drew a clean cloth from the drawer, dampened it, and laid it over the bowl, then carried the dough to the porch and set it on a table in the sun.

At each step, I silently congratulated and hated her. Maybe "hated" is too strong—but my envy and sorrow were wide and deep. I held clenched fists between my thighs.

"Will you go to town again?" I asked.

She hesitated. "I think I will. Maybe to the Methodist church this time, Roland and me."


The next morning, as we worked, Emma told Dora, "Ruby says you went to church with Moses. If you ever wanta go with Henry and me, you're welcome."

"I think I'll get Roland to go."

"Well, if he's ever tied up, come across the road."

Eventually Dora would replace me in Emma and Henry's world. Self-pity wrung my insides.

Later, I turned to Whitman, but he offered no comfort. Whitman would tell me that I was impossibly shallow or selfish. He would say, look around; the world is full of beauty and friendship and books. And all that was true, but it wasn't enough. It wasn't the warm, solid body, the loving words, the singular, requisite love.

At the same time, I couldn't stay here to suffer like Prometheus to be chained upon the rock—my heart, not my liver, daily devoured.

Friday evening, Emma cooked my favorite dinner, a beef roast surrounded by potatoes and carrots and onions, Indian

pudding for dessert. She let Jake in on our secret, since I would
be gone the next day. We told him that I had a deathly ill great-
aunt in Illinois. That much was true, though I certainly wasn't
returning to Illinois because of her. Nothing Professor Cromwell
had written indicated that she cared a fig about my welfare or my
whereabouts. Even calling her "Aunt" seemed incongruous.

After dinner, Emma said, "We've got a little going-away present for you," and she disappeared to the bedroom. Returning,
she carried a tiny box covered with blue velvet.

Handing it to me, she said, "You will come visit, won't you?
You gotta promise." I nodded, holding back tears, and opened
the box. Inside, wedged into white satin, was a small gold ring
with the initial *R* on a engraved shield.

"Put it on," Emma said. "I wanta make sure it fits. But first,
look inside it."

I tipped the ring to read, "Remember us." And then I wept.
Would there ever be an end to the weeping?


Professor Cromwell and Mrs. Bullfinch were seeking a room
and employment for me. A rooming house might be best for my
lodging. I had enough money to see me through until I found
work and, thanks to Emma, I had skills to offer. I could work in
a restaurant or hotel or laundry. I could even be a housekeeper,
if I wasn't thought too young.


Saturday morning was a wrench of separation, of doing each
thing for the last time, gathering eggs, tossing grain to the chickens. Jake had already milked the cows, but I visited them before
he let them out of their stanchions. I would miss the icy mornings with them, our breath clouding together in the air.

Emma packed food for me in an old carpetbag, enough to

feed me for several days, though I would reach Beardsley the next afternoon. Henry drove the three of us to town in the automobile. Again, my mind took photographs of everything: the two farms; the cemeteries where the orphan dog had roamed and Lily Allen was buried; and dusty Main Street, bustling with town people at their shopping, in and out of Lundeen's Dry Goods, Rabel's Meat Market, and Kolchak's Dray and Livery.

At the depot, I gave Emma the remaining photograph. "If there's anyone you think would like it," I said. Then I told her and Henry that I would come apart if they lingered over goodbyes. They nodded and, with much employment of handkerchiefs, they left me on a wooden bench in the depot, with fifteen minutes remaining until my train departed. Since the passenger car was not full, I had a double seat to myself. I sat at the window and looked down Main Street, hoping to catch sight of Henry's Model T, but it was lost among buggies and wagons and other automobiles.

The blessed thing about trains is that they rock you to sleep, and I fell into a doze of tears and fatigue, lying across the seat, my head pillowed on my bag. It was early afternoon when I woke and we were in Iowa. The Iowa border being no more than a few miles from Harvester, it was not surprising that the landscape looked exactly like the country around Harvester, flat prairie divided—neat as pins, Emma would say—into farms and groves and lakes.

As I stared out the window, one farm would strike me as resembling the Schoonover spread, another the Allen place. I viewed the countryside through those lenses on the way to Beardsley. Were these trees as lovely as the cottonwoods in Henry's grove, trees that spoke in whispering-sibyl voices, trees he'd told me were of the *deltoides* variety? Henry knew things like that. *Deltoides.*

. . .

The next morning, as we approached the outskirts of Chicago, the train slowed—by regulation, the conductor told me—and I could see how huge the city was. Few people I'd known in Beardsley, apart from my parents and Professor Cromwell, had ever been to Chicago. Mrs. Bullfinch had dreamt of it, she said, but it hadn't come to pass, not yet.

I had to change trains and railway stations in Chicago, something that hadn't been necessary on my earlier railway trips. I wasn't frightened. At each step, people were kind.

I would have liked to spend more time in the city, more time than I had between trains. Maybe one day. In my dreams I would wander the city with Roland. We'd explore the place where the great World's Fair had been, and we'd swim in Lake Michigan.

The crowds dizzied me in their numbers and their scurrying. I didn't think I'd want to *live* in a place where you had to rush so, but I wouldn't mind a visit to look around and take in all the . . . *differentia*, yes, that was the word.

Despite their pace, the people looked perfectly normal, and those who helped me were perfectly friendly. It was reassuring to know that. Most people from little towns and farms thought city people were different in some indefinable but probably negative way.

When I was settled on my second train, fortunate again in a double seat, I was exhausted but pleased to know how to make the transfer. In my dreams, again, I'd be able to show Roland, and he'd be impressed by my sophistication.

Though the train was moving, we were still in the city, and the clicking of the wheels was quieter than it would be when we reached the country. The conductor had taken my ticket and I was rummaging through the food Emma had packed. I wasn't hungry, but neither did I want Emma's kindness going to waste. Maybe someone else would like a sandwich.

Across the aisle, a young woman was gazing out the window. She was red haired and tiny, barely five feet, I would guess. And though I couldn't see her face, her figure and movements said she was probably about my age. As we finally left the outskirts of Chicago behind, she turned away from the window and I saw that she was pleasant looking, with a happy smile.

"I'm Alice," she said.

"I'm Ruby," I said. "I have so much food. Could you eat a sandwich or an apple—or both?"

"I'd love a sandwich and an apple. I only had toast and coffee. We had to hurry. My Aunt Alice—I was named for her—was afraid I'd miss the train."

"You live in Chicago?" I asked, digging out a beef sandwich and an apple and handing them to her, along with the napkin Emma had included.

"Oh, no. I live in Winstead. I've been visiting my aunt in the city." She set the apple beside her on the seat, unwrapped the sandwich, and took a bite. "This is delicious. I can't thank you enough. Aren't you going to eat?"

"I'm not hungry."

I gave her time to eat, then asked, "What do you do when you come to Chicago? I was just between trains. I've never been in a city before."

"Well, this time," she began, and her voice and face were awash with delight, "I came to buy a wedding dress."

"Oh my." I didn't want to hear any more. My eyes filled and I dug into my bag for a damp and wadded handkerchief.

"Did I say something wrong?"

But I turned away and lay my head down. When the train reached Beardsley, Alice had already left, folding Emma's napkin beside me.

# CHAPTER TWENTY

Professor Cromwell was waiting on the platform as the train pulled into Beardsley. Serena had once described him as a natty dresser—nothing flashy, but neat and fashionable. This autumn afternoon, he wore tan wool trousers, a tweed jacket, and a driving cap cocked at an angle. As I alit, he removed the cap and came forward to shake my hand then grab the two carpetbags, one with the food, the other, clothes.

"I have a little trunk they'll be unloading from the freight car," I told him. He nodded and we walked down the platform to where the freight wagon stood. As freight was being lowered onto the wagon, I pointed out my trunk. The man in charge picked it up and followed us to the parking area at the end of the depot, Professor Cromwell indicating his automobile—a Cadillac roadster, he told me. I admired it. It was sleeker and more light-hearted than Henry's Model T. Roland would love it.

"You gave up your buggy," I said.

"No, I still have it. Also the horse," he told me as my trunk was loaded onto the back of the roadster. "The Cadillac is fine for town, but if I have to drive into the country, I still prefer the horse, at least on the roads around here," he continued, handing me into the automobile.

Since the top was down, I fished in my bag for a scarf. The town looked bigger than I remembered. "How big is Beardsley?" I asked.

"Twenty thousand or so, I think."

The streets were brick or granite setts, a few paved, so that dust didn't rise around us as it did in Harvester. Still, my heart was hundreds of miles behind me.

"Where are we headed?"

"As you wished, I found you a rooming house. It's near Mrs. Bullfinch and the house where you lived. I thought you'd like that."

Indeed, it was on the same block as my little house and Mrs. Bullfinch's! Though on the opposite side of the street and several down. A big white clapboard, it had an open porch that reached around three sides, where rockers, some wicker, some metal, lined up, so many maidens waiting to dance.

A Mrs. Lander—slender, gray haired, and well kept up, with the melting blue eyes of a fairy godmother—was the owner, and she met us at the door, greeting us with considerable warmth. "Professor Cromwell, *so* good to see you again. And this must be little Ruby." She took my hand and gave me a searching look, as if she could divine some important element of my character by studying my face. And perhaps she could if she'd been in the rooming business many years. "That is how Professor Cromwell referred to you. He wanted a big, pleasant room for 'little Ruby.'"

Letting go of my hand, Mrs. Lander turned to lead us up a carpeted open stairway, saying, "You are in luck, my dear. Professor Cromwell rented the room for you *just* as Miss Hoover was moving out. Miss Hoover was with us several years, so we were all exceedingly pleased for her when she found a nice el-igible widower, Mr. Hardwick. And she didn't have to change her monogram. Very clever of her to hunt down a fellow with her same last initial."

As we rose up the stairs, I noted that the hem of Mrs. Lander's challis dress ended several inches above her instep. An up-to-date woman was Mrs. Lander.

We came to the turning in the stairway where a stained glass window cast a rosiness across the landing. Up three more steps and we were in a long, wide hallway carpeted like the stairs.

"We have electric lighting here—a great advantage. You will share a bathroom, of course," Mrs. Lander informed me. "As I have six of you young ladies—I don't take men—I had a second bath put in. In a rooming house, that's quite a luxury. Many places, you still have to use an outhouse. So uncivilized."

Indoor plumbing was the luxury, as far as I was concerned, though I would have traded this cushiness for a room near the rock elm with a chamber pot.

On the center of each door we passed was a tiny metal frame holding a card with a name printed on it. "Ann Borden," "Susan Westerby," "June Rezmerski."

"And this," said Mrs. Lander, sweeping into the last room on the right and gesturing broadly, "is what I call the Princess Room. As I told Professor Cromwell, it is my largest and airiest and has a little balcony overlooking the backyard."

Everything was clean and tidy, probably as Mrs. Hardwick, née Hoover, had left it. An imitation Axminster carpet awash with cabbage roses covered the center of the room.

"I'll go down for your trunk and bags," Professor Cromwell said and left us.

"He's a lovely man," Mrs. Lander noted.

"Yes. He was an old friend of my parents."

"He can't be all that old."

"Twenty-eight, I believe." All I wanted was to be left alone to throw myself across the bed and be homesick.

"Handsome. A bit of premature gray in the temples, but I always think that looks distinguished."

I opened the door to the small balcony. The backyard was mostly grass, bisected by a brick path leading to a small barn.

"You could do worse," Mrs. Lander observed.

"Yes, it's a very nice room." I turned away from the yard.

"I meant Professor Cromwell."

"I don't understand."

But then Professor Cromwell was carrying in my trunk. "Where would you like this, Ruby?"

I pointed to the foot of the bed.

When he had left again to fetch the bags, Mrs. Lander continued, "He paid the first month's rent. He didn't want you worried about money."

"He shouldn't have done that. I can afford the rent."

"Oh, don't misunderstand. He was very proper about it. Professor Cromwell is a gentleman."

Had she been vetting him? Did she check up on the male friends of all her young ladies? I was to learn that Mrs. Lander was an inveterate matchmaker. That struck me as odd, for if she were successful, it would mean constantly replacing her tenants.

"The asters are beautiful," I said, pointing to a bouquet on the chifforobe.

"Those are from Mrs. Bullfinch. She brought them over this morning. She hoped you'd come for lunch tomorrow."

Professor Cromwell came in with the two bags, and Mrs. Lander excused herself, saying, "I'll let you get settled, then."

"It must be hours since you ate. May I take you to dinner?" When I looked both exhausted and dubious, he said, "I'll have you home early. A quick dinner, and then home to sleep."

*Home*, it wasn't. But Professor Cromwell had been kind and generous. Saying no would have been rude and ungrateful.

"I'd like to freshen up," I said, like a girl in a society novel.

"I'll be back in an hour." At the door, he turned. "Mrs. Lander insists that male guests and escorts should be met in the parlor, so come downstairs when you're ready." He smiled and was gone.

I dreaded dinner. I was sure that Professor Cromwell would want to know all about Harvester and the Schoonovers and the Allens. My heart was too raw to discuss any of that.

I needn't have worried. Professor Cromwell—"call me Barrett"—did nearly all the talking, telling me about his classes at the college and the laboratory work he was doing for commercial hire.

When I asked who his clients were, he named an Oklahoma oil company and a Pennsylvania foundry. "I enjoy the lab work," he confessed. "Maybe too much."

"Maybe you should work for a company that has its own lab."

"Maybe someday, but right now I cherish my independence. If I don't like the commission or don't approve of it in some way, I can say no."

"Your commissions paid for the roadster?" I asked, hoping he wouldn't find the question impertinent.

"Oh, yes." He cast me a speculative look. "Speaking of employment, I've found you a job at the college. In the administrative office. Nothing exciting, I'm afraid. Mostly filing and attending to records, but it'll pay your way. I hope you won't find it too dull."

"It's work. That's what I need. Thank you for your trouble."

"No trouble," he said. "You won't start till the beginning of the month, so you have a few days to catch your breath and reacquaint yourself with Beardsley."

Over dessert, which I refused, he said, "You've become a young woman since your parents' funeral. What a terrible day that was, most of all for you."

"I still talk to Serena and Denton. I ask them for advice. But they don't answer so often as they once did. You understand?"

"I hope I do. I want to," he said with warmth. He continued, "To me, they were an example of something . . . *sterling*. Nothing I can really define, but something . . . well, you see, I truly can't find the words." He sipped his coffee.

"I kept as many of Serena's books as I could," I said. "They're in my trunk."

"I discovered that when I carried it up," he teased.

"I read them to keep in touch with Serena and Denton. And because I enjoy them. I read her Whitman—it was audacious of Serena to read him, don't you think?"

He nodded.

"Some of the poems I agree with heartily, but I find him re-petitive at times. Repetitive and, well, explicit. I'm not shocked—I've been living on a farm. Farm life is explicit. Animals are an-imals, but I've wondered about Serena, if she was shocked or what she thought."

Professor Cromwell waved to the waiter for more coffee and asked if I minded if he smoked. When he had lit a small cigar, he said, "Your parents were extraordinary. Not at all what one expects of small-town, Midwest folk. I don't know where that came from. As far as I know, they were both from Ohio, some community like Beardsley, maybe. But they were open to ideas, to different ways of looking at things. Their kind aren't easily shocked, except by cruelty.

"Your great-aunt still refers to them as 'Bohemian.' I wouldn't have a quarrel with her on that account except that, in this part of the world, 'Bohemian' connotes something jaded and anti-Chris-tian, and that would never describe them." He laid aside his napkin. "I don't remember Serena mentioning Whitman, but, if she had, I doubt it would have been with shock. Serena was like a beautiful child, wide-eyed and full of wonder."

Had he been in love with her?

Back in my room at Mrs. Lander's, I opened the trunk. The photograph of Serena and Denton I placed on the bedside table.

"Well, what do you think, you two?" I looked at their happy faces. "Did I do the right thing? I've come here to be bitterly lonesome rather than stay and be utterly miserable."

Turning once more to the trunk, I extracted the cups and saucers, tea pot, sugar bowl, and creamer. I arranged them on a lace doily atop the chest of drawers.

The beautiful cowherd I hung on a nail beside the bed where I could greet him every morning and wish him good night at the end of the day. Though I'd lost the real cowherd, this one would always travel with me. I thought of Roland's words as we lay beneath the rock elm—"You're the wife of my soul"—and folded the words into the tapestry bag with the shiny clasp.

By eight o'clock, I had washed, brushed my teeth, and pulled on my Harvester nightgown. Life was divided into two parts now: Harvester and Everything Else. Eventually I'd acquire Beardsley nightgowns, but they would not compare.

I went out to the balcony, closed the door behind me, and rolled a cigarette. Would Mrs. Lander object to my smoking out here? It might give her establishment a bad reputation. But for what I'd given up, the world owed me a cigarette.

# CHAPTER TWENTY-ONE

T he night was black, but the tip of Roland's cigarette glowed orange from the back steps. From the watering trough came the clink of a handle and a small splash as Dora dipped a pail.

"Why are you hauling water in the dark?" I called.

Suddenly, from out of the darkness came a slavering panting. Again the black dog leapt at me and again I swung the spade handle. And the dog fell at my feet, as before. But this time, Roland came running. "Why did you kill him? He was only hungry!"

Hearing Roland upset, I began to weep. "I had to. I'm so sorry." I woke, aching with regret—the awful kind, for which there is no remedy, nor any end.

I couldn't go back to sleep for fear of re-entering the dream. I still felt half in it, half out. If I heard Roland shout again, "He was only hungry," my heart would turn to ash.

The sky outside the window was black. I had no clock. I pulled the chain on the bedside lamp and sat up, shivering. I'd left the door to the balcony open.

*Dear Emma and Henry,*

*The trip to Beardsley was uneventful, except for changing trains in Chicago. I was a bit apprehensive, but everyone was helpful and kind, not what might be expected in such a large city.*

*The food you packed was delicious. I shared some with a young woman who was sitting across the aisle from me, and I still had apples and carrots to munch on later. The jars of pickles and jam I'll share with the other women who live in this rooming house.*

*Professor Cromwell and Mrs. Bullfinch found a clean, attractive rooming house on the same street where I had lived with Serena and Denton! Isn't that amazing? A Mrs. Lander owns it and seems nice although I don't really know her yet. Five other young women live here, but I haven't met them. I think they are off to church this morning or are sleeping late.*

*Professor Cromwell has also found a position for me at the college. He says it's mostly filing and keeping records, but it will pay for my keep, and that's the important thing.*

*But I miss: feeding the chickens, gathering eggs, digging in the garden, milking the cows, canning, but, especially, you, I miss you. And, of course, tell Teddy I miss him and the tune he sets up whenever a wagon or buggy drives by.*

*Please greet Jake for me. Have you heard from Dennis? You know, it was Dennis who taught me how to smoke, but please don't tell him I tattled. I begged him until he finally gave in. My room has a balcony, and last night when I was lonesome, I sat out there and smoked a cigarette and somehow I felt closer to all of you.*

*Before I close, I want to thank you again for my beautiful ring. I will never take it off.*

*My address here is 557 Chestnut Street, Beardsley,*
*Illinois. Please write.*
*Love from your devoted,*
*Ruby*

I knocked on Mrs. Lander's parlor door, though it stood open. She emerged from somewhere in the back. "Ruby, what can I do for you?"

"I was wondering where to mail this letter."

"If you drop it in the basket on the table by the front door, I'll put it out for the mailman in the morning. I do that for all my young ladies. Any mail that comes for you, you'll find on that same table." She looked askance at my green cotton dress with the rosebuds, but said nothing. It wasn't what young ladies were wearing in this bigger town, perhaps.

"Will you be seeing that nice Professor Cromwell today?" she inquired.

"I'm not really sure. I thought I'd walk down the street and ask Mrs. Bullfinch what time she wanted me for lunch."

"Well, if the professor stops by, I'll tell him where to find you."

When I arrived for lunch at twelve-thirty, Mrs. Bullfinch embraced me, as earlier, like a relative long believed dead. "Little Ruby, I thought I'd never see you again, you'd gone so far away!" She fluttered a handkerchief at her throat as if the heat were perishing, though the day was cool and bright.

She seated me in a parlor armchair, then bustled off to the kitchen, returning momentarily with two glasses of red wine. "This is Italian," she said handing me a glass, then lowering herself onto an ornate settee the same color as the wine.

I must have looked perplexed, because she said, "My fiancé

brings the wine. I have several bottles in the kitchen cupboard. It's not sherry."

Indeed. It puckered my mouth. But I asked, "Your fiancé?"

"I thought I had written about him. No? Well, his name is Giorgio Lambini, and he travels, selling men's shoes. Quality, expensive. A company out of St. Louis. St. Louis is the shoe capital of the world, did you know that?"

"I had no idea."

"Yes. He spends one week a month in this territory. But when we're married, he'll move in here and operate out of Beardsley."

"Where does he operate out of now?"

"St. Louis, same as the company. That's where he grew up."

I took another puckery sip of Giorgio's wine. "How did you meet?"

"It was a hot day this past summer," she said, settling back in her chair. "You know how hot and sultry it can get here. Or maybe you don't remember, but it can." She sipped her wine. "I was sitting on the porch," she continued, "or what you might call the veranda. Over the border I believe they say 'veranda.'" She spoke of Kentucky as if it were a foreign country.

"And along came Giorgio, lugging his sample case and looking ready to shuffle off this mortal coil, as they say. He stopped at the bottom of the walk, removed his panama hat, and inquired if my husband could use a pair of the world's finest shoes. The very best leather, no expense spared in their manufacture.

"Well, a single woman doesn't tell a traveling stranger that her husband's been dead for over ten years. If you take my meaning." She waited for me to nod, so I did. Continuing, she explained, "But I could see that the poor man was ready to expire from the heat, so I asked if he'd like a glass of iced tea. You'd think I'd offered him nectar of the gods—'nectar of the gods' was one of your dear mother's phrases—actually, God rest her sweet soul. He said iced tea was the grandest offer he'd had all day.

"I told him to sit down in the wicker rocker and I'd fetch a glass. He kept saying, 'Grazzi, grazzi,' and kind of bowing. Very courtly, Italians.

"Well, that was the beginning. He was in town a week, staying at that awful hotel near the depot."

I nodded again.

"He's very fond of music. Italians are, you know. I played the piano for him and sang 'Whispering Hope,' and he wept, Ruby, he truly wept. I've always been of an artistic turn, as you may recall. I think that's what attracted him. After that, every time he came to town, he brought sheet music from St. Louis with the latest songs. And he even found a book of Italian songs with the words translated into English. We have the grandest times."

She gave her head a gay, girlish toss as she added, "Giorgio is a wonderful cook. I'm not so fond of garlic as the Italians, but, as they say, 'when in Rome.'" Her sigh was fond and reflective.

"And now you're engaged," I said. "I'm so pleased for you." I set my glass on a side table, hoping the remaining wine would go unnoticed. "When is the wedding?"

"In a year."

"Not sooner?" Having known Mrs. Bullfinch more or less all my life, I felt free to ask.

"Well, you know how it is. Giorgio has so many details to settle in St. Louis. All his family is there, so you can just imagine."

When I didn't respond, she went on, "Little Mrs. Pedersen, next door in your old house, thinks that Giorgio is stringing me along. She says, 'Imelda, serve that man his walking papers. He's making a fool of you.' She has very strong opinions.

"But Ruby, I don't see it that way. Maybe I'm too philosophical, but Giorgio brings me wine and sheet music and he cooks wonderful meals when he's here. He bows and kisses my hand and we laugh and sing and talk late into the night.

"If he was to disappear in a year, as Mrs. Pedersen says he

will, well, I say, 'Weighing things on a scale, I think there's more good than bad about the situation.' What do you think, Ruby?"

"Won't it break your heart if one day he doesn't come back?" I was not so sanguine as Mrs. Bullfinch.

"I suppose it will. Yes, I suppose it will. But what's the alternative? Serve him his walking papers, as little Mrs. Pedersen says? Fine. And then what? No wine, no sheet music, no talking late into the night?"

She rose, indicating I should follow her into the dining room where the table was set for lunch. I admired her for leaving unsaid, "I'm not young. I dye my hair, have for years. Maybe there won't be any more Giorgios." And I admired her fortitude, but, with my heart in pieces, I didn't have her philosophical turn when it came to love.

At a quarter to three, I said goodbye and started back to Mrs. Lander's, pausing in front of the house where I had lived with Serena and Denton. It was as it had been, if a bit sprucer. A boxwood hedge had been planted along the walk, and new steps led up to the front porch. This was where "little Mrs. Pedersen" lived now. One day I would knock on the door, introduce myself to "little Mrs. Pedersen," and ask if I might have a sentimental look around.

By three o'clock, I was back in my room. Professor Cromwell arrived soon after the tall clock in the foyer chimed three-forty-five. Mrs. Lander did not like having to climb the stairs to deliver messages to her young ladies; fortunately, a dumbwaiter allowed her to ring a bell and shout up to announce a guest. The dumbwaiter owned a resonance such that the very walls around it reverberated with the ding-a-ling and her "Yoo-hoo, up there!"

When I entered the parlor, Professor Cromwell was seated, visiting with Mrs. Lander. Her melting blue eyes again noted with pity my green cotton dress with the rosebuds. Mrs. Lander, I would come to understand, was a woman whose tender heart often misdirected its pity. It was hard to fault her for that.

Seeing us to the door, she said, "Here, Ruby, if you're going in the automobile with the top down, wear this riding hat." She reached for one from a hall stand. "It ties under your chin. I keep it for my young ladies." She considered. "If you were going into the countryside, I would suggest a duster as well." Still, several fingers rested on her chin in a gesture of speculation. Duster or no?

As Professor Cromwell and I climbed into the roadster, he said, "I thought you might enjoy a drive around town. Also, I have a key to the administration building at the college, so I can show you where you'll be working."

The halls of the imposing brick administration building were dim and echoing and smelled faintly of floor wax. There was a comforting familiarity about it. When I mentioned this to Professor Cromwell, he said, "You probably came here as a child with Denton. Maybe many times."

*Of course!* I remembered one such occasion. I'd sat on Denton's shoulders as he delivered papers to the office now ahead of us, the one with the bubbly glass on the upper door and gold letters that spelled something grown-up. A lady had taken the papers from Denton and told me what a big girl I was getting to be. It wouldn't be long before I would be attending classes at this college, she'd said. I'd laughed. "I'm only four years old!" I told her, and she laughed.

I turned to Professor Cromwell. "Thank you again for finding me work here. It's perfect." A tenderness filled me for the man who had connected me with my darling father.

In the drive around Beardsley, he pointed out landmarks, like the courthouse where a Civil War cannon and a statue of General Grant stood, then the hospital, and two or three churches. He pulled up in front of one of them. "The funeral for Denton and Serena was here. I've never forgotten how brave you were."

"You told me it was all right if I wanted to cry."

For a moment, he laid a hand over mine, then we drove on. We passed an elementary school I had attended, though that experience seemed a thousand years ago. Eventually, we drove around the park that formed the town square. Gales of fallen leaves scudded across the still green grass, mounding against the trellis skirt of a band shell. Several restaurants surrounded the square, a dress shop, a department store, and a stationer's.

Later, we had supper at a Chinese restaurant where murals depicted dragons and villages and mountains and oxen bearing goods and peasants. I was enchanted. Since I'd never eaten Chinese food, I asked Barrett—which he kept insisting I call him—to order for me. The chicken, vegetables, and noodles were delicious, unlike anything I'd had before: a little sweet and a little salty. The whole occasion was like a party, with the owner, Ming Ho, bringing us one thing and then another.

"I'm delighted that you like it," Professor Cromwell told me. "I thought you might."

On our return to the rooming house, we passed a high school, and Professor Cromwell stopped again, saying, "This is where Serena taught. Those windows, there at the end, on the second floor, are her room."

Some slight, unintended note in his voice revealed the answer to the small question in my mind. Tonight I would ask Serena about this.

# CHAPTER TWENTY-TWO

S itting on the balcony, I smoked a cigarette and composed an imaginary letter to Roland. As I stared through the wrought iron balusters into the backyard, Roland seemed to invite me down where the grass was neither dry nor dusty. He spread a blanket against the dew and waved, beckoning me.

But from a seemingly great distance came the sound of someone knocking. Wiping my eyes on the hem of my nightgown, I hurried in. "Who is it?"

"June from down the hall." The young woman began whistling "Shine On, Harvest Moon."

I was inclined to like a whistling young woman. I had never subscribed to the idea that it was uncouth for a woman to whistle. The one who stood in front of me when I opened the doorway looked older than me but was probably not above twenty-two or three. Her blondish-brown hair was wound into a frowzy bun on top of her head and she wore a flannel nightdress, immediately explaining, "Aunt Helen made it. 'People die of pneumonia in Illinois,' she said, as if people don't die of pneumonia in Missouri. I'm June Rezmerski, by the way. Nurse at the hospital. May I come in?"

For a moment I was confused. Did she imagine that I was ill? But no. She was simply—what was the word?—explicating.

I opened the door wider. "Of course," I said, pointing to the reading chair by the window. She handed me three cookies, keeping another for herself, and said, "My mother bakes them by the gross." She sprawled across the upholstered chair, legs flung over one arm. "Welcome to Lander's Matrimonial Agency. If you don't have a beau, never mind, Mrs. Lander will scour the territory." She bit into her cookie and went on, "You've been crying. Are you homesick?"

I winced. June Rezmerski was plainspoken. "In a manner of speaking," I told her.

She let it go at that. "Where's home?"

"Originally Beardsley but, lately, a farm in Minnesota. My parents died when I was twelve. I've been a hired girl since then. But I've come back here, and I start work in the college administration office the first of the month."

"Quite a history for someone who's—what are you—seventeen?" she asked, biting into her cookie and brushing the fallen crumbs from her lap.

I had to stop and think. "Eighteen? Seventeen or eighteen. I've lost track."

"Mrs. Lander said she guessed about seventeen. She said a 'nice, respectable gentleman' brought you here. She also said he was good-looking and a professor and twenty-eight." She glanced at me. "That right?"

"Yes, I suppose it is. He was a close friend of my parents."

She nodded. "Well, Mrs. Lander has pretty much staked him out for you. And if you don't want him, one of us young ladies should set our caps, because he's quality." June raised her brows at each quote.

That made me uncomfortable, and June took note. "Don't mind Flora. She's a pretty good old girl, just wants her young ladies to marry well and be happy."

"Where do you come from?" I asked.

"St. Louis, but I have relatives over this way. Aunt Helen found me the nursing job. She dreams of my snagging a doctor." June studied the remaining portion of her cookie. "Older women. Too much time on their hands. They wanta pair everybody off. Especially with doctors."

"My friend Mrs. Bullfinch, who lives up the street, has a fiancé from St. Louis, a gentleman traveling for a shoe company. I don't suppose you know him. St. Louis is a big city."

"What's his name?"

"Giorgio. Giorgio Lambini."

June shook her head. "No. But my uncle Bert might know of him. He works for a shoe company. I think half of St. Louis works for the shoe companies. Giorgio Lam . . . bini. I'll remember when I write."

June came from a family of seven children, four girls and three boys. "But two of my sisters are married, and one of my brothers is a bargeman."

"On the Mississippi?"

She nodded. "So there's just one girl and two boys at home."

"It must be wonderful having so many brothers and sisters."

"Except when you need the bathroom. This place is heaven." She laughed, rising. "Well, I'd better hit the hay. Work in the morning. Nice to meet you, Ruby. I'll ask about your friend's beau. Giorgio Lambini." She finished the cookie; rose, fussing a bit with her frowzy bun; and left, whistling "Shine On, Harvest Moon."


Before starting work on the first of October, I purchased three dark skirts—black, brown, and navy—and four white shirt-waists. I'd get by with the hand-me-down winter coat from Emma until I had put aside more money.

From the dry goods store I bought an inexpensive brooch and several short lengths of ribbon to wear with it. I didn't want to shame Professor Cromwell by looking like his country cousin. Also, I planned to visit Aunt, and I wanted to look like someone she'd be sorry not to know.

My first day in the administration office, I found the work much as described, but I didn't mind the sameness. Mine was the job that the woman years ago had held, the one who told me I would soon be going to college! If Denton were still alive, I might be taking test papers from him and registering the grades in one of the big black ledgers.

I worked alongside a young woman who was, I learned, twenty-five, an advanced age for an unmarried, attractive red-head with nice ways. Her name was Annie Farrell. Eventually she would tell me that her "darling boy" had died of diphtheria in Chicago a few months before they were to be married. And so I began fantasizing a romance between her and Professor Cromwell.

In her first letter, Emma wrote, "The Allens were upset because you left and didn't tell them. I explained about the great-aunt who was sick, but Roland saw through that. He came across the road to talk private. He mourned like you'd died. He was so broken up, I hope you don't mind I gave him that extra photograph of you.

"Dora asked for your address, says she wants to thank you for all you did. I gave it. I hope you don't mind that either."

Two days later, there was a letter from Dora lying on the hall table.

"I was so sad when Emma said you had left. All I could think of was the mean things I said when you came to help after my fall. You turned out to be my true friend.

"You were so clever. You knew if I learned how to work, it

would make all the difference. It has, Ruby, it has. And Emma says anything you didn't have time to teach me, she'll take care of."

As I had known Emma would.


"Your great-aunt wants to see you," the professor said. We were sitting on a bench in the square, beside the band stand. The November wind raced, scudding clouds across the sky.

"Good. I was hoping for an invitation."

He looked surprised. "I'd have thought you'd dread a meeting."

"Ever since I left Beardsley, Aunt's dislike has bothered me. It makes no sense. If most people like you," I said, "and there's one who doesn't, that one is a burr under your saddle. You can't rest until you know the why of it. At least I can't. Did she ever tell *you?*"

"Your name hasn't come up unless I mention you." He said nothing for a minute. "If you call on her, you should know that age and bad health have drawn her claws. She's bedridden, dying."

"You said as much in your letters."

I remembered the snow, the thick loveliness of it, the great mounds of it. "Serena would never have left me with Aunt that night if Mrs. Bullfinch had been at home. But Imelda was visiting her sister."

Withdrawing a cigar from the inside pocket of his jacket, Professor Cromwell lit it slowly, protecting the flame from the wind and taking time to consider. "You remember that?"

"I remember everything about that night. Aunt huffed and stewed when Serena asked if I could stay for a couple of hours. When they weren't back in that time, she told me how thought-less and inconsiderate they were, how they reminded her of her despicable brother, Hiram—Serena's father. I slept on the sofa, and when a man came the next morning to tell us they'd been found dead, I swear Aunt looked relieved. They wouldn't bother her again."

"I'm sorry."

"I was twelve, so Serena and Denton could have left me at home. I suppose they were overprotective. Somehow I feel partly responsible for their deaths, though that makes no sense—they'd have frozen no matter where I was." The afternoon was graying into premature evening.

We sat silent, the professor smoking. At length, smudging out the cigar beneath his heel, he said, "My experience with her has been very different from yours. Maybe she's changed."

I waited a week, then knocked on Aunt's door on a Saturday afternoon. Beatrice—she who starched and stretched the lace curtains—answered. I introduced myself and told her, "Aunt said she wanted me to call."

The shadowy sickroom was fetid and close. The wallpaper was sepia, and its leafless branches clawed upward toward out-of-the reach sunlight. Aunt sat upright in bed, old-fashioned mobcap on her head, crocheted shawl around her shoulders. Six years had passed since our last encounter and, even in the semidarkness, I could see that those years had done her no kindness. She was gaunt and ashen. Beneath her many brown liver blotches, the blue veins on her hands and temples stood out like rivers on an eerie topographical map. On the bedside table was a small framed picture of someone I assumed, from his halo, must be a twentysomething Jesus.

"So you've come," she said, her voice stronger than I'd expected. "Sit there where I can see you." She pointed a skeletal finger at a straight-backed chair in the room's one sunlit spot, the bow of a bay window next to the street. With the light falling full on me, I felt like the accused in the box.

"Professor Cromwell said you wanted to see me."

"I wanted to see what you've made of yourself." She reached for a glass of water on the table and sipped, wiping her lips on a lace-edged handkerchief. "You've been working as a hired girl, the professor tells me. On a farm." She sucked in air. "You liked it there." Returning the glass to the table, she asked, "Why'd you come back?"

"I wanted to be near Serena and Denton," I lied.

"They're long dead."

"The people we love are never entirely dead to us, are they?"

"You sound like your mother," she told me. "My own people, back in Ohio, are entirely dead."

"That's too bad. The dead can be a comfort."

She allowed herself a single cackle, then coughed, and sought to clear her throat, though something still rumbled in her chest like distant thunder. At length she said, "The dead can be a comfort, you say. And can they be a discomfort?"

"I don't know."

"Perhaps you'll find out." Her blue lips twisted in a near smile, though the words were not intended as pleasantry.

For several minutes neither of us spoke. Finally I leaned toward her. "Why did you dislike Serena?" I asked. I did not add, "And why do you dislike me?"

She considered for a moment. "Serena had been spoiled. Both parents doting. Like so many who're spoiled, she assumed that everyone would love her. Well, I wasn't about to. Such people lack character."

"I don't understand."

"We're supposed to struggle," she said with a kind of impatient patience, wondering where my brains were. "To be forged in the fire." Her hands clenched in twiggy fists on the matelassé spread.

"And were you forged in the fire?"

"I was."

"And . . . those who are forged in the fire . . . are they kinder for it?"

"You're too bold. That's your mother. Her father—my brother, Hiram—was the same. Lacked good sense. Took his own life when the going was rough."

"I expect I'm like my mother and Grandpa Hiram in many ways—probably in ways you most despise."

"Have you got any religion?"

"Only a little." I'd show her I had enough character or brass to speak my mind. "Mostly I believe that everything is holy. People and birds and trees and dirt and manure, sun and moon. That probably comes from working on a farm."

"Pantheism."

I was amazed she knew the word. "Yes, I suppose."

"Pagan."

"Maybe."

"And what *isn't* holy in your pagan view?"

I had to think. "Cruelty."

"You have a simple mind."

"You may be right."

"The true God is a jealous god. He doesn't brook holy suns or moons or . . . manure." She cackled again, then fluttered the handkerchief, an impatient gesture to *shoo* the cough away.

"I don't want to know that God. It's on account of manure," I explained, "that you have good things to eat and flowers in your garden."

She was tiring, I could see. I was exhausting her with my "boldness." But I wanted to know something. "What is your illness?"

"I'm rotting from the inside." Her grin was macabre.

"Rotting?"

"My organs are eating themselves up. He's forging me in the fire again."

"God?"

"Who else?"

"But why? Why is he punishing you?"

"It's not punishment, you silly thing! It's a privilege."

I shuddered. "That's grotesque."

"Not at all. My suffering is a sign."

"Of what?" The conversation was increasingly bizarre yet somehow compelling.

"I've been chosen."

"What does that mean? Chosen for what?"

"To sit beside Him when my young face and body are returned to me. When I am as I was at eighteen." The hand clasping the handkerchief rose and fell again and again, in a slow rhythm, as if she spoke in iambs. Then she stopped beating time and put her hand to her cheek. "I was a high-strung beauty. 'Like a thoroughbred race horse,' Papa once said. I'll be that girl again when I go to Him." Her mood was drifting from confrontational to dreamy, and I wondered if she were on laudanum or some other opiate.

"And what will you do when you're sitting beside Him?"

She roused. "I'll serve Him."

"Serve Him what? I imagine He has everything He needs."

"I'll serve Him love," she said, her voice coy. "I'll be His bride."

Perturbed, I rose. "I think I should go."

"Yes . . . that would be good." Veined lids closed over unfocussed eyes swimming in their sockets.

I had already reached the bedroom door when she rallied. "You'll come again." Not an idle invitation or mere suggestion.

"When?"

"Tomorrow."

Once the front door closed behind me, I stood on the porch waiting for the return of reality. The old woman had led me into a dim realm of . . . what? Religious hysteria?

And I still didn't know, not really, why she disliked me and Serena.

. . .

When we were settled at Ming Ho's, Professor Cromwell asked, "How did it go?"

I shivered. "Does she talk religion with you?"

"Only to the extent that she wants me to read her the New Testament." He sipped from a steaming cup of tea. "Is that what you mean?"

"No. I mean does she talk about going to meet *Him*, as she puts it, when her young face and body are returned to her?"

Flicking his napkin across his lap, he looked up. "Her young face and body?"

I nodded. "I know we're supposed to get our bodies back at the end of time, but, well, she made it sound . . . I can't even explain."

"I should have gone with you. I'm sorry I talked you into the visit."

"She wants me to come again tomorrow."

"I'll go with you."

"No. Whatever she has to say, I think she'd hold back if you were there."

"That's the whole point in my going—so she'll hold back."

"As unpleasant as it will be, I have to hear it." He looked dubious. "It's to do with my family. She hated her brother—my grandfather. That much is obvious. If I understand correctly, which I probably don't, it carried over to Serena and now me. Anyway, I need to know the rest, even if it does mean listening to her creepy meditation about heaven."


Sunday morning I wrote to the Schoonovers and Dora, enclosing affectionate greetings for Roland. Affection!—what a bloodless, milksop word. I smoked a cigarette on the balcony, then carried the letters downtown to the post office.

The day was bright and inviting, so I wandered till I found a little cafe off the square and took a seat by the window, indulging myself with a pastry and coffee. The sun shone warm through the glass, and I felt as lazy and cossetted as a cat on a sill. I kept a small book of Keats in my bag—bits and pieces, odes and sonnets—and as the cafe was not crowded and the morning was one for Keats, I took it out.

Opening it at random, I met these lines:

*Can death be sleep, when life is but a dream,*
*And scenes of bliss pass as a phantom by?*
*The transient pleasures as a vision seem,*
*And yet we think the greatest pain's to die.*

Later, climbing the stairs to Aunt's bedroom, I was glad for the hour I'd had in the cafe. Keats's passion and sympathies had sweetened my mood and I felt ready to beard the beast. In the bedroom doorway, I straightened my shoulders.

"So you've come," Aunt said, echoing the previous day's greeting and opening her eyes. "Well, come in, then." She pointed again to the straight wooden chair in the oriel. "Have you been to church?"

"No. I've come from coffee and pastry and reading poetry in a cafe."

"Do you ever deny yourself pleasure?"

"Not if it doesn't hurt anyone." But did we always know?

"Sin is sin, whether or not it hurts people. It hurts our Lord."

"By 'our Lord' you mean Jesus?"

"Who else would I mean?"

"I'm never sure when people say 'our Lord' if they're referring to the Father, the Son, or the Holy Spirit." How had we gotten into this?

"They're all our Lord, but I've taken Jesus as my personal lord. We're very close."

"Does He talk to you? I mean, you said He assures you of His love."

Aunt looked up at me with mistrust under half-lowered lids. Was my question some form of sophistry? If so, "Are you planning to marry Professor Cromwell?" she asked out of the blue.

"No."

She nodded. "Just as well. He's a cultured man." She flourished another one of her handkerchiefs.

"I agree." I shifted in the chair, gazing out the window at late November where a man across the street dug old leaves from under denuded shrubs. From the stuffy unreality of this room, he might as well have existed on another planet. "Tell me about Ohio," I said.

"What about Ohio?"

"Where in Ohio? Columbus? Cleveland? I don't know for sure."

She coughed into her handkerchief, then struggled to rearrange the pillows behind her, buying time. I crossed to the bed, plumped the pillows, and handed her the water glass from the table.

Gathering her wits, she sighed, a deep, grum sigh. "Originally, home was Crawfordsville, east of Columbus. Known—not very far nor very wide—for the healing water and mud. A mucky little cave outside of town, closed up half the year. Desperate cases, one's who'd tried better places without luck, came for a last crack at a cure."

Despite the sounds in her chest, Aunt seemed stronger today, more focused. Though she paused frequently for breath, she appeared intent on continuing.

"My family had money. We weren't much affected by the terrible war. In fact, Papa's little factory was doing well."

"Did my grandfather—Hiram—serve in the war?"

In a voice rich with disdain, she said, "No. An accident cost him his left hand. His own fault." She laid her head against the pillows and closed her eyes.

I hadn't known that my grandfather had lost a hand. "How old was he, when that happened?"

She opened her eyes, slowly, as if the question wearied her beyond my imagining. "Sixteen."

"Did he use the healing mud?"

As before, something at the back of her rheumy eyes leapt out, then was gone. She hesitated. "I forget," she said, fussing with the matelassé spread, smoothing it on either side of her thin legs.

I wanted to know more about my grandfather's hand. It was a terrible thing to lose at any age, but especially at sixteen, when you were coming into your powers. Emphatically, I said, "It would seem natural that he'd use the healing mud."

The mobcap threatened to come off as she shook her head. "You're exhausting me," she hissed, dismissing my queries with a wave of the handkerchief. "You'll kill me." She closed her eyes again.

"You told me that God's the one killing you. He's forging you in the fire." I was goading her, and I was only a little sorry for it. "I want to know about my grandfather."

I sat stubborn on the chair, waiting as slow minutes passed. Downstairs, a clock chimed three. In Aunt's throat, phlegm wheezed. She probably expected me to leave, *wanted* me to leave.

At length she said, "I'm not obliged to tell you any of this."

"Yes, you are. I'm family."

"Not *my* family."

"I'll keep coming back until you tell me what I want to know." I rose to go. "Why do you hate my grandfather?"

Without opening her eyes, she said, "Maybe another day.

Maybe not. I don't make promises." She smiled expectantly. "Tomorrow, He may come for me."

Once again I stood on the porch, filling my lungs with cool, cleansing air. The man across the street had gone indoors, and now a golden light shone from his front windows.

# CHAPTER TWENTY-THREE

The following Saturday, when I arrived, Beatrice told me that Aunt was sleeping. "She took her medicine early," she said.

Though a cold rain fell the next morning, I repeated the previous Sunday's routine: a walk to the post office, coffee and pastry at the cafe off the square, and a return to Aunt's. Once there, I followed Beatrice into the hall, handed her my umbrella, and mounted the stairs. Intensified by dampness, the odor in Aunt's room was heavy and sweet-sour, as I imagined death smelled. The old woman appeared groggy and faraway, only lifting a hand off the spread to acknowledge me. When had she taken her "medicine"?

Crossing to the chair, I inquired, "How are you feeling?"

"Deathly sleepy." Though mucose and labored, her voice was impatient. How did I *imagine* she was feeling?

"I won't stay," I said.

"Sit." Imperious even in her torpor. "You wanted to know more, and I've decided you shall."

"Your brother, Hiram, lost his left hand in an accident," I prompted. "*How* did he lose the hand?"

Her glance was venomous, and I shrank from it. She sat up straighter, bony breast heaving with emotion. Her hand shook as she reached for the water glass. After she'd sipped, she slammed the glass back on the table, drops flying. I'd struck a nerve still raw after three score years.

Ignoring my question, she cried, "The story begins earlier—*my* story!" She struck her chest with a fist. "Papa came home to tell us he'd met a young man named James Jasperton. James had come from Connecticut hoping the mud would relieve a war wound he'd suffered the previous October, and Papa had invited him for dinner that evening. 'The man was wounded at Ball's Bluff,' Papa explained. That had been a massacre of Union soldiers in Virginia."

Perspiration stood out on Aunt's forehead and clung to her brows. I rose to blot the moisture, but she brushed me away.

"After several dinners, Mama and Papa were so taken with Captain Jasperton, they invited him to move into our guest room while he was 'doctoring' at the cave. 'After all, the man's a hero,' Papa said.

"James was with us all that spring and early summer. He took a great interest in Papa's button factory, often visiting him there. Perhaps he saw himself running it, years hence." Pausing, she glanced with fondness at the picture of Jesus on the table.

"James Jasperton was courtly. Not so handsome as some but more prepossessing than most. We were all impressed when he related the dreadful scenes at Ball's Bluff and what he'd endured there, including the gunshot wound. He tried to spare the ladies' sensibilities, but I wasn't shocked. Death and gore didn't bother me. I wanted to know everything that had happened to him.

"He played the piano and had a marvelous baritone. In the evenings, we gathered in the parlor and sang sentimental songs. We were all smitten with James. You couldn't help yourself." Her voice was fervid but growing weak and thready. Eyes closed, she lay her head back. I wondered if, behind those eyes, she was see-ing Jasperton as he had been. Downstairs, the hall clock struck the half hour. In the street outside, a child rolled a hoop through petering-out rain.

Just when I thought Aunt had fallen asleep, she said in a low voice filled with decades of regret, "As you may have guessed, James and I fell in love. We planned to marry, though we hadn't yet told Mama and Papa." Angrily, she hissed, "We should have eloped." Then she did fall asleep. Suddenly and deeply.

I wasn't done with Aunt. I sensed that we had come close to the heart of it. This was one last thing I could do for Serena—and for myself as well.

The next Saturday, as I took my place on the chair, I said, "Aunt, you haven't answered my question. How did Hiram lose his hand?"

"Have the courtesy to let me tell my own story." Despite mortal illness, the old woman could instantly call up anger. *Her* story, never Hiram's.

"It was June. Mid-June. A lovely morning full of birdsong. Though his wound vexed him, James insisted upon walking the mile or two out to the cave. While he was there, I took the buggy for a drive. When I returned, I left it in the road in the event it was needed in the afternoon."

So smoothly did her story unspool, so letter-perfect was she, I knew that Aunt had been rehearsing it, probably daily, since that long-ago June.

"Looking forward to mealtime conversation with James," she went on, "Papa had come home to eat. Your grandfather, Hiram, was late returning from an errand to the post office. Then sud-denly he was there, rushing in, breathless and wide-eyed, letting the screen door slam and holding his side as if he'd run all the way. 'It's James,' he blurted. My heart seized. Had something had happened to James?

"Mama said, 'Sit down, Hiram, catch your breath.' Finally he told us he'd seen a wanted poster outside the post office with a picture that looked exactly like James. But the wanted man's name was Jacob Johnson. He had killed a teller in a Missouri bank robbery gone wrong, and he had been wounded there. It wasn't known if he'd survived.

"The moment Hiram finished his story, he took off for the cave. When he returned, he told us James had already begun the walk home, and fled across the fields when he saw Hiram coming.

"Papa threw down his napkin. 'Hiding somewhere till the next train!' he cried. He'd been duped and he was furious."

Suddenly, Aunt was gasping and hacking. I half-rose but she put up a hand. I sat on the edge of my chair.

Even as she quieted, the rattle in her chest was louder. Eventually, she rang the bell sitting beside Jesus on the bedside table. When Beatrice appeared, Aunt asked for more water and her medicine. When this was done and Beatrice had retired, the old woman grimaced, putting a hand to her middle where her insides were consuming themselves. Still I waited.

After some minutes she asked, "Where was I?"

"James . . . Jacob had taken off when he saw Hiram."

"Heartbroken, I cried out and ran from the table. Father tried to grab me, but I flew out the front door, Hiram close behind. 'Bertie,' he called, 'don't go.' But nothing could stop me. I had to find James. We would run away—wherever.

"I jumped into the buggy and cracked the whip. Hiram screamed, but I didn't stop. His hand must have caught in the spokes."

I stifled a moan.

Flecks of spittle appeared at the corners of Aunt's mouth. The bones and cords of her neck stood out like a delicate mechanical construction.

"You must rest," I told her, crossing and laying a palm on her restless, flittering hands.

But she was not done. "Mama and Papa never forgave me," she whispered. "'You heard your brother scream,' they said. 'Hiram nearly bled to death, there in the dust, in the road. And for what? For a murderer!' They wouldn't see *my* side, *my* pain. Everything was about Hiram—but it was all Hiram's *fault*, stupidly running into the road!

"Days of sitting at Hiram's bedside, not knowing if he'd survive the infection, sickened them against me. They couldn't look at me. Papa sold the factory and they moved to Columbus, but not before setting me up, away from them, here in Illinois." She sighed. "I never saw James again. Hiram did me out of my love and my family."

I stood at the foot of the bed. What could I say? *Some things that are meant to be can never be?* I understood the desperation of what she'd felt for Jacob Johnson, but her hatred of her brother—that I couldn't understand.

Then she began to cough and couldn't stop, her body convulsing with spasms. I went to her. Her breath was foul.

My God, how she clung to life.


On my final visit, she held to her breast the picture of Jesus, calling him James. Before I left, she motioned me to the bed. I bent close. "I wanted someone to listen," she whispered. She was done with me.

I had served her purpose, someone who asked, someone who listened. And she had served mine.

Rest well, Serena.

. . .

As it transpired, the old woman had more days remaining to her than I'd have guessed. Despite her dismissal, I half-expected a summons, but I did not hear from her again, although memories of our sessions visit me in odd moments. Something about sin unatoned for.


The war in Europe ground forward. England entered on the side of Belgium and France. President Wilson was committed to American neutrality, but we held our collective breath. Professor Cromwell was convinced that we must inevitably be drawn into the conflict. "We're like kissing cousins, we and the Brits. We couldn't allow them to fall to the Kaiser."

Dora wrote, "I worry about the war. Do you think Roland would go? What would I do?" I told her no, I didn't think Roland would go. He had a farm to run. But the possibility of his going was worrying.

The year drew to a close, and the Lander house emptied as her young ladies headed home for Christmas. Even Mrs. Lander herself departed, leaving behind a box of homemade divinity for me: *I don't like to think of you alone at the holidays. Of course there's the professor, but still . . .*

The night before she left for St. Louis, June came by, whistling "Jingle Bells" and handing me a tin of her mother's sugar cookies. "She sent them especially for you." They were delicious but not so heavenly as the molasses ones from Emma.


The week before Christmas, I scoured the stores around the square searching for a gift for Professor Cromwell. Finally, at the stationer's, I chose a pen and a box of elegant stationery, not unlike that on which he'd written me in Harvester.

Those few days alone in the Lander house, I imagined living in such a space with Roland—how we would decorate for the holidays, carrying in evergreen boughs and holly from the backyard. The rooms would smell of greenery and, when I baked, cinnamon as well.

More than once, I sat on the sofa in the living room and imagined Roland in the nearby armchair, reading. He would turn a page, look up smiling, then set the book aside and take my hand, leading me up the stairs. In this way, I drove myself mad.

Professor Cromwell invited me to Christmas dinner at Ming Ho's, the only open restaurant for miles around. "For orphans and strays," the professor said, and it was a full house of orphans and strays under the cutouts of Santa and Jesus and angels and deer and camels and kings and President Wilson and Abraham Lincoln cheek by jowl with the Chinese villagers and cloud-capped mountains on the walls.

Ming Ho did not serve alcohol, but Professor Cromwell and others had brought bottles of wine or flasks, and Ming Ho turned a blind eye as pots of tea were laced with rye. When we had emptied the tea from our cups, Professor Cromwell poured white wine into them, joking, "I suppose I might be accused of leading a young lady down the garden path." He raised his cup.

"After a long day of feeding threshers," I told him, "we would occasionally indulge." I lifted my cup and sipped. "I have already set foot on the garden path."

When most of the gathered had finished their meals and were nibbling almond cookies, a friend of the professor's, a young biology instructor, stood in the aisle between the booths and began playing carols on a viola. One after another, his audience started to sing along.

Whether rye-induced or prompted by a song's sentiment,

more than one eye grew misty as the afternoon wore on. Misty eyes notwithstanding, for me, this was the jolliest Christmas since St. Nicholas had left a china doll with fur-trimmed coat under the tree.

Before the professor settled our bill, we exchanged gifts: from him, I received a gold-famed cameo. "It looks like your mother," he said.

Each week of the new year, I expected to hear that Aunt had died, yet she clung on. Finally, on a particularly dark and bitter Saturday afternoon in late January, Professor Cromwell showed up at the rooming house. Mrs. Lander rang the little bell and called up the dumbwaiter, "Yoohoo, Ruby," but not in her usual cheerful voice.

When I came downstairs, Professor Cromwell was sitting in the parlor with Mrs. Lander, their faces grave. Mrs. Lander spoke first. "Professor Cromwell has unhappy news, Ruby. I'll leave him to tell you."

"Your great-aunt has died," he said, "and her lawyer contacted me, thinking I might know how to locate you."

"Why me?"

"I don't know. He said he'd be in touch. In any case, the funeral is Wednesday at the Church of the Covenant. Ten a.m. I thought I'd attend. I'll come for you."

In my room, I paced, pursued by Aunt Bertha: admonishing me to keep my feet off the furniture, sit up straight, stop chewing my cuticles, stop whistling, stop touching the lace curtains, stop humming, and stop being five years old, or six, or seven.

But no. That was behind us, surely. I had listened. It was over. Serena was vindicated. She had tried her best.

. . .

Once Serena told me that the summer after she graduated from high school, her own mother had drowned when a ferry boat sank on Lake Erie. Her mother had been visiting a friend in Cleveland. At first, Serena's father seemed to cope, she said, and life went on. But as weeks passed, he blamed himself for not accompanying his wife. He lost weight and grew forgetful. He stopped shaving or going to church.

Serena was away at school. Aunt Bertha came to look after Hiram—but instead of looking after him, she aggravated him, and he grew worse. He began wandering away. Eventually he "fell" from the top of a building in downtown Columbus. Serena never suggested that Aunt had driven him to it, but she did tell me, "Aunt should have been more respectful of his grief."

Of Denton's family I knew nothing. He'd been raised by relatives when his parents were carried off by . . . good God, I couldn't recall what. Taken *in toto*, we were an ill-favored family.

Never, since Serena and Denton's funeral, had I felt so alone. But why now? I didn't mourn Aunt. Still, I did want to be part of a family, and we could have been one, if she'd chosen. We could have been a foundation to stand on. So I went to her funeral and I mourned for the family we hadn't had.

In the vestibule afterward, a gentleman in a serious blue suit approached us. "Professor Cromwell," he said, extending a hand and nodding in my direction, "is this Ruby Drake?"

"It is."

"Miss Drake, I wonder if you'd pay me a call . . . you work at the university, I understand . . . say, Saturday afternoon?" He handed me a business card.

Nonplussed, I took it.

"It's about Miss Bertha Berryman's—that is, your great-aunt's—little estate," he explained.


Late that Saturday afternoon, I sat in Mrs. Bullfinch's parlor. "He says my great-aunt left me her house and a bit of money." Accepting a glass of bad red wine, I told her, "The rest of her money went to Beatrice, the woman who took care of her, and to the Church of the Covenant. I don't know what to make of her leaving me anything at all."

Mrs. Bullfinch clasped her hands in a flutter. "First of all, I'm thrilled," she said. "Second of all, I suspect that the professor had a finger in this pie."

"What do you mean?"

"He used to call on your aunt, as I'm sure you know. He's a kind man and lonely. Plus he thinks the world of you. He probably praised you to your aunt, and maybe she had second thoughts about the way she treated you and your darling mother."

I couldn't buy that. "I don't know," I said, "that's very *Pollyanna*." I paused; perhaps Mrs. Bullfinch was a fan of Eleanor H. Porter's novel. "What I mean is, it doesn't fit the Aunt Bertha I knew."

Mrs. Bullfinch sipped her wine slowly and, adopting a philosophical tone, said, "People change."

She set her glass down and leaned in. "I remember how Eugene—Mr. Bullfinch—got religion toward the end. He'd always been a holiday Christian, and now here he was wanting to say the rosary every night. The rosary! We weren't even Catholic." She shook her head in wonderment. "People can change when they get worried about their souls."

All this made me qualmish. "I'm not sure it's right to take advantage of that."

"Take advantage of what?"

"Of people growing weak and vulnerable toward the end. It seems unethical."

"Oh, Ruby, now you're being silly." She took a quick gulp of wine. "If a person feels remorse for unkindness, shouldn't we honor that remorse?"

Now and then, Mrs. Bullfinch said something quite intelligent, even if it was misplaced. If Aunt had truly had a rational reason for including me in her will, it was this: I had listened.

I was not to take legal possession of the house and belongings till the middle of April. For this I was grateful. I had feelings to sort out and plans to make. Besides, mid-April would mean the dogwood and forsythia would be in bloom—and lilacs, too, perhaps?

# CHAPTER TWENTY-FOUR

And indeed, everything was in bloom. Yet, despite the professor observing, "This is the adventure you've needed," I was unsure.

For one thing, I didn't quite believe the inheritance. I half-expected that someone had made a whopping mistake, and that the house would end up with the Church of the Covenant.

For another thing, saying goodbye to Mrs. Lander was more difficult than expected. I'd grown fond of my landlady over the last six months. Though I was only moving a few blocks away, she clung to my hand as if I were sailing to the Sandwich Islands.

"You must promise to stop by often," she said, fussing with a loose strand of hair. Her melting blue eyes said she was happy for me; inheriting a house and a bit of money was an outcome nearly as sunny as seeing me married to a good prospect.

The actual moving of my worldly goods from 557 Chestnut to 864 Beech was half an hour's work. The lawyer had said I could air the rooms and do some cleaning a week before the move, so when Professor Cromwell carried in my trunk and bags, the house was ready. Well, temporarily. I planned many small changes.

"Do you want this at the foot of the bed?" The professor stood in the front hall holding the trunk.

"Yes," I said and led the way up the stairs. I'd chosen the big front bedroom, with the bay window overlooking the street. I wasn't bothered that she had died in the room; I wasn't superstitious in that way, and the electrified streetlights pleased me. I wanted to look out at the night and see them shining like so many moons lined up just for me.

This house was nearly as large as Mrs. Lander's, too large for one person. I had already talked to Annie Farrell at the college about moving in, and I would need one or two roomers in order to afford the place. As a single woman of property and responsibilities, I had to consider such matters. The money from Aunt would only keep things going for a year or two.

After returning to the house from Ming Ho's that evening, the professor glanced at the windows. "How do you feel about the lace curtains?"

"What an odd question."

"I know you had unhappy memories of them."

I smiled. "I'm thinking about voile." He laughed. He really was a comfortable and pleasant man. And when Annie moved in, he and she would often be thrown together.

"He's in love with you," Mrs. Bullfinch had recently assured me.

"You're wrong," I'd said. "He was in love with Serena. I remind him of her. What he feels for me is just a reflection of that love." She looked unconvinced—but, frankly, I didn't consider her the best judge of matters romantic.

Later, as the professor was leaving, he took my hand. "I see happy days ahead for you." He bussed my cheek. "I hope I'll be a part of that." Well, of course he would be; we were good friends.

After I saw him out the door, I went to the kitchen pantry and found a hammer and a jar of nails. I ran up the stairs and flung open the trunk to retrieve the painting of the cowherd: *Darling Roland, you will live beside me all my life.*

The photo of Serena and Denton went on the bedside table. Next, I removed the tea set from the trunk and carried it downstairs to its new home in the parlor. I cleared the low table by the front window, straightened the doily, and laid out the pieces of china beneath a lamp with a stained glass shade. How it all sparkled. Oh, Serena, if only you could see. And one day, in Aunt's backyard, there will be a gazebo. Correction: in *my* backyard.


Even during the first days when I wasn't entirely convinced it was mine, I was like a child arranging and rearranging doll house furniture. I did pull down the lace curtains on the first floor, replacing them with ivory voile. I could do nothing about the like-new brown velour parlor suite, since Aunt had rarely used the parlor. But, at a Catholic church bazaar, I found a couple of pillows with burnt-velvet covers in shades of brown and a soft moss green. They mitigated the elephantine sofa.

The biggest change, however, was in scraping off Aunt's dark red wallpaper in the parlor and dining room. The pattern of large, unidentifiable blooms and vines was not merely ugly, it was minatory, menacing. A constant reminder of Aunt Bertha.

I had no knowledge of wallpapering, but when I'd finished removing the old, scooping it up in armfuls and carrying it to a barrel in the backyard to be burned, I hired a woman from the neighborhood recommended by Mrs. Bullfinch. Mrs. Heidebrink accompanied me to the paint store to choose new wallpaper, and we returned home with a refined pattern of pale green stripes on ivory. Two days later, the parlor and dining room were bright and fresh.

In the big bedroom, the sepia wallpaper with tortured limbs gave way to yellow tulips in beribboned bouquets. Aunt's ghost

did not haunt my bedroom or my house, even if she did sometimes hector my mind.

864 Beech was gradually becoming entirely mine. Mine
and Roland's. Everything I did, I did for Roland. Every room I
walked through, I walked through with him: imagining him repairing the screen door on the back porch; eating fried chicken,
sitting at the kitchen table; digging up crocus bulbs; and, later,
making love in the front bedroom, the giant moon in the sky and
the smaller ones on the street limning our bodies in the darkness.


Emma wrote, "On account of the war and demand for crops,
Roland is paying off his farm debts. He even bought a tractor.
But he's working too hard.

"Anyway, he's glad to be getting out from under. I have to
say tho that some of the spunk's gone out of him. Do not blame
yourself, little girl. You did what you had to do. Some things that
are meant to be can never be. You know that."

If Annie Farrell hadn't brought home a prospective roomer
that evening, a young woman named Delia McDuff, who worked
in the dean's office, I would have blubbered for hours. "Some of
the spunk's gone out of him." What exactly did that mean? For
the first time in weeks, I dreamed of the wild dog.


Annie moved in on the first of June, taking the back bedroom
overlooking the garden. For all her faults, Aunt had kept the
yard attractive, with azaleas, mock orange, peonies, and lilacs
that were grown to small trees. Along the west fence lay a plot
that must once have been a kitchen garden. I would plant carrots
and beans and a few other vegetables there.

Beside the house, to the east, a gravel drive led to the little barn
where a horse and buggy were no longer kept. The walls inside held

garden tools and, above the stairs, a hay mow housed a jumble of cast-offs. Investigating, I found a standing birdcage; a couple of mismatched dining chairs; unaccountably, a cradle; a wardrobe trunk; also unaccountably a dusty bisque doll of German manufacture; and a long, narrow mahogany table, suitable for the front hall.

On the first of July, Delia moved in, selecting the bedroom next to Annie's. Only one bedroom remained vacant, and I decided to leave it that way for the moment.

From the built-in dining room buffet, I chose a silver tray of Aunt's, placing it on the hall table, à la Mrs. Lander. "For incoming and outgoing mail," I told Annie and Delia.

And then another letter from Dora arrived. "Ruby, you can't imagine how hard we are working. I told Roland a while back that I want a baby, but he said not now, now we have to work, we have to pay off the debts. And we are paying them off. By this time next year, we'll own everything free and clear. It's a weight off Roland's mind, and off mine, too, I suppose.

"You say you have a well behind the house. Just like us! Only you have running water in the kitchen instead of a pump. That is so GRAND. And a real bathroom with running water! It takes my breath away.

"Emma is good to me. Almost like having a mother. But I still miss you. You are my sister. If we weren't working so hard here, I'd come visit. I could help you water the garden.

"I have to bring the clothes in off the line now and start supper. I'm sending you love. This afternoon I carried sandwiches and muskmelon out to the field and told Roland I was writing you. He said to be sure to send you his love."


On the third of August, when Emma could have little time for writing letters, one arrived. I tore it open immediately, praying that nothing had happened to Roland.

"Hold onto your hat, Ruby. We took two boys. They are brothers. David and Solomon. They came into Harvester on one of them orphin trains from back east.

"They are a handful but good. And it's sad how grateful they are to be took. And by folks who will adopt them if they don't behave too bad. I can't wait for you to meet them.

"These two take the place of two of the babies we lost. Roland has always taken the place of the other. Old God does move in mysterius ways.

"The boys pitched right in, gathering eggs and such. They want to know everything about farming. I get tired just answering questions. I can see that I am going to fall in love. Henry too.

"Let me tell you, sister-in-law Hermione was jelus when she saw what good lookers the boys were once we got them cleaned up and into some new clothes. Henry was *that* pleased."

It was like a miracle, if you believed in miracles. David and Solomon. Two biblical heroes. I wrote at once to congratulate Emma and Henry, then sent each of the boys a book of Greek mythology and a Horatio Alger. Within days, thank-you's arrived in the mail, containing the appropriate number of cross-outs and smudges.

Harvester life had gone on without me. Something perverse in us does not want the other life we have known, the life back *there*, to alter. If we should ever return, we want it to be as it was, to reenter it as if we'd never left. For a few days, I was melancholic.

The time had come to purchase headstones for Serena and Denton's graves. The stonemason lifted his brow and then smiled when I gave him the two quotations. For Serena: "O, she doth teach the torches to burn bright." And for Denton: "A woman would run through fire and water for such a kind heart."

Professor Cromwell accompanied me the day the stones were

laid. A breeze blew and the sun shone, heedless of the occasion. Each of us was silent, occupied with our own recollections and questions.

Laying a bouquet of lilies on each grave next to the professor's roses, I wondered how well I had known Serena. We'd been close, but a child can never fully know a parent. And I'd had only twelve years.

Serena had been a good deal older than Barrett Cromwell— thirty-seven when she died—but that meant nothing. We love whom we will. Had she recognized that he was in love with her? Had Denton? Had there been accommodations, tensions?

We were still silent on the ride back to town. At the house, he dropped me with a nod that was an afterthought, while I barely remembered to wave.

# CHAPTER TWENTY-FIVE

While a war raged in Europe, the summer of 1917 passed quietly in Beardsley. Folks read about the war in the newspaper, of course and orators on speaking tours exhorted us to get involved but, unless we knew someone who'd enlisted or a mother who'd lost a son, life was rather disconcerting in its sameness.

Then Emma wrote to say that Dennis had signed up and would probably be sent to France if the Allies didn't win soon. And according to the *Beardsley Journal*, that wasn't going to happen.

Dennis's enlistment unsettled me. I was fond of the overgrown boy. I asked Emma to send a military address for him, and when it arrived, I prevailed upon Annie and Delia to add their greetings and observations to my letters. It became a competition among the three of us to see who could come up with the drollest or most intriguing tidbits.

I told Annie and Delia how I had coaxed Dennis into teaching me to smoke. They began ragging him about dragging a good woman low. Now that I was in my own home I smoked as I pleased but on the back porch.

Delia was a seemingly shy little thing—too shy to flirt with men and almost too shy to speak to them—but something about writing to a faraway stranger revealed another woman. She began gathering jokes and entertaining newspaper items. Finding one of Finley Peter Dunne's books at the secondhand store, she cut out his Mr. Dooley columns and sent them to Dennis. By October, it was clear that Dennis would not mourn the loss if Delia became his sole correspondent from our household.

Annie and Delia tended to eat dinner at Dandy's, where I often joined them. On one such evening, Delia confessed, "Dennis asked me to send a photograph of myself. What should I do?"

"Send him one," Annie said.

"Why wouldn't you?" I asked.

Discomfited, Delia blushed, mumbling something about being a mouse.

"That's silly," Annie said.

But Delia went on, "I'm someone that people forget having met."

Annie and I burst out laughing.

"It's true," Delia insisted. "It's partly because I'm shy, I know, but it's also because I'm—well—I'm like a piece of very ordinary furniture. Like a school desk, say. Utilitarian. Nothing satin or velvet."

"Do you *want* to be satin or velvet?" I asked, surprised by the turn the dinner conversation had taken.

"Maybe not satin or velvet, but not quite so utilitarian, either. Utilitarian eyes, utilitarian mouth," she said with mild disgust. "Freckles, even."

"You have beautiful skin," I said. "Smooth and soft as a peony petal."

"And a lovely mouth," Annie added. "Plus, you have quite a nice figure. Don't you ever take these things into account?"

"Really, you ought to have a photograph taken for Dennis. For the war effort," I teased.

"What would I wear?"

Now the floodgates were breached, and Annie and I deluged Delia with suggestions. On the walk back to the house, we promised to go with her to the photographer the following Saturday, after dressing her and arranging her hair.

And so it was that Delia McDuff and Dennis Cansler became sweetheart correspondents over the next year. And Annie, Delia, and I grew into a little family of sorts.


Despite the riches of my new life and the continuing kindness of the professor, my mind was always layered, with Roland underneath it all. I had been gone from the farm for a year now. I'd never imagined that the pain would lessen in a year's time. And it hadn't.

As Emma had once advised in a particularly intimate letter, "You put one foot ahead of the other, little girl. And hope that someday they carry you to a high and peaceful place." I continued to be amazed at words spoken and written by people who considered themselves quite ordinary. But then I'd always known there was nothing ordinary about Emma.

As for Annie and Professor Cromwell, he defied my best efforts. He was always cordial to Annie, and a casual friendship did develop, but it lacked the heat I'd hoped for.

On Annie's side, I felt a reticence. But why? The professor was intelligent, ambitious, good company, and perhaps a bit of a blade. Girls took physics, I was told, only because he taught it. And according to college gossip, more than one had set her cap for him. I refused to believe, as Mrs. Bullfinch maintained, that Barrett Cromwell was in love with me. If I believed that, a weight of obligation or sadness or mindfulness would lie on me, undermining our friendship.

In the meantime, I continued writing imaginary letters to

Roland, telling him, *No words but your words, no mouth but your mouth* . . . Hadn't I read somewhere that doing the painful but right thing had its compensations, that you felt good about yourself? For me, where Roland and Dora were concerned, that was not true.

I was sorting laundry in the dining room when I heard mail falling through the letter slot. From the foyer carpet I fetched a smudged envelope with no return address but a Harvester postmark. When I tore it open, a snapshot fell out. Dim, as on a cloudy day, but clearly discernible, Roland stood by the Schoonovers' gate. On the back, scrawled in pencil: the words "I live on hope." *But "hope" of what?*

Autumn came and went. A letter from Emma described the threshing season and how they had lost one or two good workers to the military. Dora herself had worked in the field alongside the remaining men. "She's determined to see the Allen place out of the red. Roland worries me with that tractor, going too fast, doing too much. What's the big hurry?"

At the Christmas holiday, Delia, Annie, and I had a week off from our respective offices. Since we only knew one man, we decided to throw a ladies-only dinner party. We asked Mrs. Lander, Mrs. Bullfinch, June Rezmerski, and several other friends to attend: ten in all around the big dining table.

I asked Professor Cromwell to purchase wine. He wanted to pay, but I wouldn't hear of it. This was a party for women and by women.

Everyone brought a single anonymous gift which they dropped

into a pillowcase in the front hall. Before dinner, we sat around the parlor drinking our semisweet white wine and dipping into the pillowcase to retrieve a gift. I received a small brass photograph frame and had coincidentally donated in turn an empty photograph album.

Mrs. Lander said, "You should ask Professor Cromwell for a photo for your frame, Ruby."

Looking at Annie, I said, "But Mrs. Lander, the professor and I aren't a . . . couple."

"More's the pity," she countered. "It's time you settled down."

I gestured at the room, the house. "I have a job, I have a home, I have good friends. Some other woman will have to pluck the professor off the tree of romance."

"Oh, Ruby." She sighed maternally and sipped her wine.

Rising, I said, "Bring your glasses to the table."

"How daring, to serve wine," Mrs. Lander said as we herded into the dining room. "Though I do love it, I admit. Very European."

I could hear Mrs. Bullfinch telling Mrs. Lander how her friend Mr. Lambini brought red wine from St. Louis. "He was sorry to be tied down there in St. Louis for the holidays. Meetings of the salespeople, he said."

June caught my eye, shaking her head slightly.

"He's so fond of Beardsley," Mrs. Bullfinch went on. "Says the restaurants here are every bit as good as in St. Louis."

And then we were taking our seats. Delia had created place cards for everyone, decorating each with a watercolor pine bough. As we were finding our places, and with St. Louis on her mind, Mrs. Bullfinch asked, "Did anyone here visit the Exposition in 1904? My late husband took me. It was so grand. Unimaginable. I still think about what a good time we had. We took the train. Only twice I've been on the train—going to and from the Exposition."

The Exposition was a popular topic in Beardsley, despite

being thirteen years in the past. So little of historical moment
happened there, folks clung to those memories that rose above
the ebb and flow of daily life. Flora Lander and her late husband
had made the trip. He'd bought her an amethyst bracelet and
they'd eaten ice cream out of twisted waffles.

And June Rezmerski remembered how thrilling it had been
to be a child, actually living in St. Louis during the Exposition.
"I was six years old. We went on the streetcar four times to see
everything."

For our dessert, Annie had made a Lady Baltimore cake.
"You went to so much trouble," one of Delia's friends exclaimed
as Annie carried it in on Aunt's stemmed cake plate. "The one
time I tried, I made a dreadful mess of it. All those layers! Mine
kept slip-sliding in every direction."

Before the dinner party broke up, we each had another glass
of wine, toasting "our boys at the front." As the other guests were
leaving, buttoning up coats and dashing out into a light dusting
of snow, June held back.

I closed the door on the last and turned. "What is it?"

"It's about Mr. Lambini. I know it's been almost a year since I
told you I'd ask about him, but when I did, my uncle didn't know
him or anything about him. But he did write the name down. Then
recently, he was riding the street car and sitting next to a woman with
two little kids. They got to talking and somehow it came out that she
was Italian, so my uncle asked, did she know a Giorgio Lambini?
Know him? She was his sister. Why did my uncle want to know? He
said he'd heard a pal mention a friend of his by that name.

"Well, she said, she was feeling awfully sorry for Giorgio and
his little family. Giorgio had lost his job, and with the holidays
coming, it was hard.

"'Lost his job,' my uncle said, 'that is hard luck.' Yes, she
said, especially since another little one was on the way.

"Uncle Lou said that with the government buying thousands

of shoes and boots for the army, and all the shoe companies hiring, Giorgio Lambini must have done something pretty bad to get himself fired."

"Poor Mrs. Bullfinch."

"Do you think she'd want to know?"

"I'm pretty sure she wouldn't," I said as June grabbed her things from the coat stand. "I'll try to find out if he's been in touch with her."

Months passed, riding on the rails of routine. Living with Annie and Delia was comfortable. We fit together well. Our long string of evenings was punctuated by concerts and plays at the college, now and then a lecture.

One Saturday morning in March, as we sat at the kitchen table eating oatmeal, Delia said, "We should drop in on Mrs. Bullfinch." She and Annie knew what I'd learned from June Rezmerski, and we suspected Lambini had not made a recent appearance.

The morning was chilly along its edges, but the sun shone with a will, and we wore only sweaters over our dresses. By afternoon, we could shed the sweaters to dig in the spring garden.

As we approached Mrs. Bullfinch's house, we heard her playing the piano, thready soprano declaring, "Whispering hope, oh how welcome thy voice."

"Isn't that sad?" Delia knocked.

The playing and singing ceased, and Mrs. Bullfinch opened the door. "What a lovely surprise!" She ushered us in. "I was just practicing. I never know when I'll get a call," she said, leading us into the parlor. "Weddings. Funerals. Different occasions, I used to sing at least once a week around town. Now, it's once in a while. Usually for an old friend's funeral."

She pointed us to the sofa and chairs. "But that's life, isn't it? It grows smaller as we get on." Still on her feet, she said, "I'll put the coffeepot on. It's a treat having company. I don't have as much as I used to. But that's life too. Friends move in with their children or they lose their wits and go off to a nursing home, or they pass on." She left us.

A mist of loneliness rose from the furniture and Axminster. The three of us sat silent, hands in our laps, each wrapped in her own brown study. I looked into an abyss of onlyness, of being just *one*, forever. And then it passed and Mrs. Bullfinch was carrying in a tray of coffee cups, cream, and sugar.

We all rose to take the tray from her. Annie was first there.

Mrs. Bullfinch said, "I'll fetch the pot and the plate of cookies," and turned to leave again.

"I'll get them," Delia told her.

Mrs. Bullfinch acquiesced and plopped into an armchair. Picking up the conversation where it had earlier left off, she said, "I've lost another dear friend, I'm afraid. Mr. Lambini. Well, he was more than a friend. We were engaged." She took the cup Annie handed her, waving off the cream and sugar. "I think he must have died." She set the cup beside her on a table and dug a handkerchief from the bosom of her dress. "I haven't heard from him since December. If he were alive, he would write. I've thought of inquiring about him at the shoe company. I don't know what to do."

As she lifted her arm to dismiss the cookie plate, I noticed for the first time that she had lost weight. The skin on her arm hung loose.

She glanced around at the three of us, as if for advice. Sipping coffee and chewing shortbread, we cast about for something helpful or heartening to say.

None of us wanted Imelda Bullfinch writing to the shoe company. Her romance with Mr. Lambini had been naive and silly and pitiful but to have it shattered absolutely by news that a Mrs. Lambini existed, one with two children and a third on the way, was unthinkable. She so needed her illusions intact. Mr. Lambini might be her last commercial traveler.

Delia set her cup down and wiped her lips with a tea napkin. "I have such a strong feeling," she said, leaning toward Mrs. Bullfinch and taking her hand, "you might call it an intuitive image, that Mr. Lambini is dead. I have always been . . . intuitive. I don't want to hurt you, but I feel that you are seeking the truth."

Mrs. Bullfinch nodded, wiping her eyes with her handkerchief.

Delia went on, "I see him carrying a case . . ."

"His samples."

". . . carrying a case and crossing a busy street. He is hurrying toward a railway station . . . he doesn't notice the streetcar bearing down." Delia stopped abruptly. "Oh, dear." She tightened her grip on Mrs. Bullfinch's hand. A moment passed. "That's . . . that's how he died. I'm sure of it."

Annie and I were transfixed. For a brief second, I really believed that Mr. Lambini had fallen under a streetcar as he hurried toward the train that would carry him to Beardsley.

Tears washed away Mrs. Bullfinch's uncertainties. She smiled wanly, saying, "My dear, you don't know the comfort you have given me. I sense that you have a great gift, and you have used it to show me the terrible truth, a truth I had not wanted to accept."

Speaking to us all, she said, "I'm so glad I didn't write to the shoe company. It would have been more painful receiving this awful news in a cold business letter."

We nodded and ate our cookies. I noted that Mrs. Bullfinch finally took one as well.

# CHAPTER TWENTY-SIX

A s we headed home, Annie told Delia, "You were astonishing. Are you . . . intuitive?"

"No more than anyone."

"Well, you nearly convinced me," I said.

The next evening I stopped by Mrs. Lander's to tell June about Delia's performance.

"Tell Mrs. Lander that Mr. Lambini died," June said as I was leaving her room. "She'll begin searching for a suitable replacement."

In the foyer, Mrs. Lander waylaid me to inquire about Professor Cromwell. "I worry about him," she said.

"Why on earth?"

"Well, it's obvious he's lonely." Her expression had never been more melting. "You know, lonely men often fall prey to, well, the wrong kind of young woman."

"I don't think you need to worry. He's kept busy with his inventions and teaching. Besides, Annie and Delia and I invite

him along when we're going to a play or a concert." I pulled on
my sweater. "If you want to worry, worry about Mrs. Bullfinch.
Mr. Lambini died."

"Oh, dear! In St. Louis?"

"Yes. Fell under a street car."

"How horrible!"

I left her with that to occupy her Sunday evening.


Our happy news of the summer of 1918 was the engagement
by overseas mail of Miss Delia McDuff to Mr. Dennis Cansler.
Annie and I threw her a little Sunday afternoon engagement
party, inviting Professor Cromwell; Delia's boss, Horatio
Barnes, dean of students, and his wife, Minette; Mrs. Lander
and Mrs. Bullfinch; and Delia's two friends from our holiday
gathering. Delia's parents, who lived in Peoria, were unable to attend, her mother indisposed with an ear infection. Despite their
absence, the gathering was festive. Prominently displayed on the
dining room table, along with platters of ribbon sandwiches and
little cakes, was a photograph of Dennis in his uniform, stalwart,
handsome, and owning perhaps a bit of swagger.

Writing up the occasion for the *Beardsley Journal*, Mrs.
Lander noted, "Among the many lovely gifts received by the
bride-to-be were a beautiful silver tea service from her parents
and an exquisite linen tablecloth with a dozen matching napkins
from Dean and Mrs. Horatio Barnes."

As the dean and his wife were leaving, he told me, "I have
fond memories of your father. He was a solid instructor and a
good family man. I recall seeing him in the halls after classes, you
on his shoulders, the two of you singing some ditty and laughing." He cast a wistful glance at his wife. "We were never blessed
with children, but I used to think that if we had been, I'd want
to be a father like Denton." He took my hand. "I hope you will

find such a man." Though the words were spoken to me, his gaze strayed over my shoulder.

The world was determined that Professor Cromwell and I should be paired. However, the world had no knowledge of Roland. Heaven forfend. And the world would never understand. Nor would Annie and Delia; they might feel called upon to sympathize, but their secret hearts would not approve.

In the kitchen, stacking dishes beside the sink, Mrs. Bullfinch confided, "Dear Mrs. Lander introduced me to a widower of her acquaintance. Very nice. Rode with Teddy Roosevelt in Cuba. Lovely head of hair. And you won't believe this, Ruby, but he sings in the Congregational choir." By the color in her cheeks, I took this last to be significant.

Aunt's mantel clock had chimed five-thirty when the last of the guests wished us a good evening and headed out into a warm and fragrant Beech Street. When we'd cleaned up in the kitchen, Delia said, "Let me read you what Dennis wrote in his last letter. I want to know what you think, Ruby. You know more about his situation back in Minnesota."

She returned, reading aloud as she came, "'I've always wanted to be a farmer. But, since I've been over here, I'm having second thoughts. Mostly it's because I see how important even a county-seat newspaper can be. And how much we need them—all newspapers, big and small.'" Delia sat down on the sofa, tucking her feet beneath her, and read on, "'Would you hate living in St. Bridget, Minnesota, married to a newspaper editor?

"'Another reason I'm thinking seriously about this is because my dad is having heart problems. He didn't tell me. He wouldn't, but a cousin who lives in St. Bridget wrote me. She said he was even in the hospital a couple of days.

"'Let me know what you think.'" She folded the pages and looked at me.

"What *do* you think?" I asked her. "Can you see yourself married to a small-town newspaper editor?"

"More than I can see myself married to a farmer—though I would have done that."

"That settles it," I said.

"Just think," Delia said, "if you still lived near Harvester, I'd get to see you sometimes. I'd have a friend in St. Bridget County."

Delia left us then to write Dennis. "He'll want to know all about the shower and how impressed the dean was when I told him that Dennis's father owned a newspaper. Small-town newspapers, the Dean says," and here she mimicked his voice, "'are the cornerstone of democracy.' Imagine!"

I felt no qualms about Delia's future with Dennis. He was a young man of substance, and she would do him proud. With her "unplumbed depths," she would handle Dennis's father.

Annie fetched herself and me another cup of coffee and a plate of leftover tea sandwiches. We unlaced our Sunday shoes and sat in the parlor.

"I shouldn't eat," I told her. "Professor Cromwell's coming at seven to take me to Ming Ho's. I tried to beg off, but he said he has news."

"Maybe he'll ask you to marry him."

"Oh, don't say that."

"Don't you think you could be happy with him?"

"I don't know if I could or not, but I don't love him that way." I nibbled the edge of a sandwich.

"Could you learn to love him?"

"What if I didn't? It would be cruel to him and awful for me. He's too good a man for that."

"He *is* a good man, Ruby, and it's unkind not to let him know that he's out of the running. Tell him." She set aside her coffee cup. "But remember," she said, "he has everything girls hope for. A reasonable-minded girl would fall in love with him. If not at once, then in time." Choosing another ribbon sandwich from the plate, she added, "I bet he's a good kisser."

"I know you're right," I told her, "but I'm not reasonable, and there's the end of it." I rose and headed for the stairs. "Anyway, I think you'd make a better partner for him."

"You're wrong," she said from behind me. "Since Michael died, I've learned to appreciate my independence. I talked to the dean about college this afternoon." I heard her start up the stairs. "I'm not a reasonable-minded girl, either."

Knowing she'd love news of Dennis and Delia's engagement, I wrote Emma, adding, "Dennis has decided to take over the newspaper after all. He says that what he's seen in the war makes him realize how important papers are. He's marrying the right girl! Delia's smart and wise. She'll probably end up with her own weekly column."

Professor Cromwell and I settled into a booth with a pot of green tea and two small cups in front of us. The steamy aroma of tea, garlic, and ginger was both exotic and genial. Ming Ho's always made me feel like a world traveler.

"Now then," I said, sliding Professor Cromwell's cup toward him. "What's your news?"

"I've been offered a position in Pittsburgh heading up a laboratory for Standard Oil. I've told them I couldn't possibly accept until the end of the academic year. I've signed a contract to teach, and it's too late for the school to find a replacement."

"And so . . . ?"

"They said they'd wait. I was dumbfounded." He spoke with hurried excitement. "I've done laboratory work for them, so they know me, but I never expected anything like this."

"I thought you enjoyed your independence."

He winced, smiling sheepishly. "I have enjoyed it," he said. "But I'm looking down the road." He picked up his cup, started to say something, then set it down, looking at me.

"If this is what you want, then for heaven's sake, grab it," I said.

He paused. "It'll mean relocating to Pennsylvania," he said.

"Pennsylvania's not the back side of the moon. Would you really mind relocating?"

Ming Ho laid menus before us, and conversation was deferred while I ordered my usual chicken and vegetables and Professor Cromwell his beef and noodles.

Ming Ho, being the soul of discretion, did not linger to ask after our health. Instead of rushing forward with his story, the professor stared after the owner.

*Is he going to ask me to marry him?*

And was I a fool, as Annie had implied? Studying his face, so serious—the eyes dark and deep—I couldn't help wondering a little. His hands, resting on the table, were capable and strong. His voice when he spoke was cultured. Little wonder students fell in love with him.

At length his gaze abandoned Ming Ho and turned to me. "I'm going to ask you something, something important to both of us. I think I have a right, but I don't know what your answer might be. In any case, I don't want an answer now. I want you to take time to consider." Again, he hesitated. "You've probably guessed that you mean a great deal to me. Strange to say, perhaps, but you've *always* meant a great deal to me, even when you were a child. I hope that doesn't sound disgusting."

"No. I understand."

He reached for my hand. "What I'm saying—badly—is: please consider the possibility of marrying me." He added at once, "Don't say anything. Think about it. Will you do that?"

His face entreated, and I nodded though I already knew the answer.

# CHAPTER TWENTY-SEVEN

A boy, maybe sixteen or seventeen, ran into the administration office, breathing hard and holding his side. It was a Wednesday in October. I would remember.

"Ruby Drake?" he inquired after he'd caught his breath. I crossed to the counter that separated our desks from the reception area.

"I'm Ruby Drake. Can I help you?" He thrust an envelope at me, asked me to sign a form, then turned and left as abruptly as he'd entered.

"That's a telegram," Annie said, rising from her desk, concerned.

*Something's happened to Roland.* Ripping it open, I read, "Roland dead (stop) Tractor accident (stop) Funeral Saturday Methodist church ten a.m. (stop) Love Emma."

Annie caught me under the arms and shoved a chair beneath me as the world spun. "Put your head between your knees," she was saying. Then, to a student assistant, "Fetch Professor Cromwell."

*You are the wife of my soul,* he'd said.

I didn't see Annie retrieve the telegram from the floor, nor did I see her read it. Time passed. Someone came hurrying with smelling salts. Later—maybe minutes, maybe an hour—the professor was there, leading me out of the room and the building, handing me into his Cadillac. He'd collected Delia on the way.

"Delia will pack for you while I go pack for myself," he said, as much to Delia as to me.

Together they ushered me into the house and to a chair in the parlor, where I sat insensible. Later, they guided me out and back into the professor's automobile, Delia remaining behind. Only vaguely do I recall boarding the train. Long afterward, Professor Cromwell told me that I fell asleep immediately. I do recall waking when we reached Chicago and had to remove ourselves to another station. On the second train, I stared blindly at passing landscapes. My palms bled where my nails dug into them.

Professor Cromwell had apparently wired ahead to reserve rooms, for when we arrived in Harvester early Thursday morning, someone from the hotel met us.

Sleeping, I dreamt again of the wild dog and of Roland crying, "He was only hungry!" I woke weeping. "I'm so sorry. So sorry." I was still sobbing when Emma knocked and entered.

She sat on the side of the bed, weeping too, holding me, rocking and murmuring, "I'm so sorry, little girl." When finally she came into focus, I saw that her eyes were swollen nearly shut. Mostly silent, we sat with our backs to the head of the bed, seeking solace in being close.

"Do you want to come to the farm?" she asked before leaving.

"Tomorrow."

She nodded.

"I want to see all of you," I told her. "I want to see the farm. Both farms."

I slumped then, too heavy to sit upright. Too sad to stay awake.

. . .

Sleeping was the only way to endure, and I would have slept Friday away, too, but while I slept, Professor Cromwell had been growing acquainted with Emma and Henry. Now he told me, "Emma needs you."

After Henry welcomed us, he went with Jake and the two boys, David and Solomon, to work the long day away. Around the kitchen table, Emma, Dora, Professor Cromwell, and I drank coffee and talked of arrangements: the Methodist Reverend Norton was officiating, and Roland would be buried in the Protestant Cemetery. Pallbearers: Henry, Jake, Moses, the two boys, and Kolchak.

Dora was wan and grave, older and more solid. She bore her limp without notice.

"Mr. Cromwell," Emma said, "thank you for bringing our Ruby home."

I sat close to Emma, my left hand on her shoulder, the connection keeping me tied to her kitchen, to Roland, to everything that made me feel real and safe and entirely myself.

Before we left, Dora asked, "Would you like to come across the road and see Roland?"

In my torpor it had escaped me that Roland might be at home, that people would be coming for the viewing, the wake. "Yes."

"Mr. Cromwell?"

Along with Emma, we followed Dora across Cemetery Road. On the Allens' back porch food was lined up on a table, offerings left while Dora had been at the Schoonovers'.

In the parlor, the open casket stood before windows temporarily covered with dark fabric. An electric lamp burned on a nearby table, casting a ghostly half light over Roland. I was grateful for the unreality: the dim, waxen figure, decked out in a serge suit, was not Roland. In my mind, Roland was out in the fields with Moses. Professor Cromwell moved close, but I felt no need of support. This body did not move me. The man I'd met in the barn, his body warm and hard—that man moved me, and all remembrance of him moved me, but not this cold figure in a satin-lined box.

I turned away, as did Dora. Together we walked through the kitchen and out into the farmyard, leaving Emma and Professor Cromwell behind in the parlor. In the strong, slanting rays of October, we halted, waiting to regain our sunlight eyes. When we were sure of our steps, Dora took my hand, leading me to the pasture.

"It was here," she said, heading toward a low, boggy area alongside a creek where the cattle liked to lie in the heat of summer. She pointed. "He drove too close to the creek. The wheels caught in the muck and the tractor went over. Roland was caught under it. Moses had gone to town for gasoline." She wiped her eyes on her sleeve. "And maybe it wouldn't have made a difference."

I put an arm around her.

"He was trying to till more land," she said, "so he could put in another crop in the spring, make more money, pay everything off. He was desperate to get the tractor paid off."

We turned back toward the house. "I wish you hadn't left," she told me. "Your great-aunt needed you, I know, but now I need you."

Over a lifetime, I have found that I remember little of funerals. I suppose I have my own thoughts and pain to attend to. Maybe most people are occupied that way.

That Saturday, as I stood next to the open grave, beneath a cold October rain that would demarcate autumn from winter, I saw a familiar but unplaceable figure among those gathered. I searched my mind, recalling after several minutes the Fourth of July picnic at the Grange Hall: John Flynn, state representative, appearing genuinely moved. The woman beside him I didn't recognize. His wife? "My third-grade teacher, Mrs. Stillman," Dora told me that evening.

As we were leaving the cemetery, Emma, at my elbow, murmured, "The Lundeens came, bless their hearts." So many small threads of connection wound around me like baling wire.

Before the day was out, the sun returned, now a winter sun. In the descending light, we gathered at the Allen farm—Dora and Moses, the four Schoonovers and Jake, Professor Cromwell and I, plus a handful of friends, including the Kolchaks and several threshers and their wives. Dora's parents were conspicuous in their absence; Roland's were ill with the dread influenza.

Food was spread on the kitchen table. Emma dished up small plates for Dora and me though she herself, I noted, did not eat. I was concerned for them both. How was Dora to run the farm without Roland?

Dora and I took our plates to the stairs, where we sat picking at ham and scalloped potatoes. "What I said before, Ruby, I meant. I wish you were here with me and Moses. There's the empty room."

"You're going to keep the farm?"

"What else *could* I do?"


A light frost dusted the countryside under a pale, dying moon as Professor Cromwell and I drove out to the farms early the next morning. Our train wasn't due until eleven, and Emma had invited us for breakfast.

The colors of the landscape were solemn, fading and deepening: golds perishing into tans, tans into dun. A misty gray seeped into it all. On the cusp of winter, the land was momentarily otherworldly, a spiderweb veil thrown over it. The haystacks were mystical, as were the raggedy corn stubble and the trees baring their souls. I drank it in like liquor.

On a day such as this I had walked down Cemetery Road toward Sioux Woman Lake and found Roland. The lake had been gunmetal, and a flotilla of loons had divided its surface, sailing south.

Here my soul was planted—in the awesome toil, the smell of hay dust, the burr of cicadas, the hoary exhale of a horse on a winter morning.

Taking our coats, Dora led us into the Schoonover kitchen, bright with electricity and smelling of bacon. While I was in Illinois, lines of electrical current had been strung from town, pole to pole, out to the nearest farms.

"What do you think of the electricity?" I asked Emma.

"I'm getting an electric flat iron. Feature that," she said as she set a platter of bacon and eggs on the table. More than once as she rounded the table, pouring coffee, Emma glanced at the professor and me. Dora followed with a platter of toast and a bowl of apple butter to lay before the nine of us.

Later, after the men had left for their respective barns, I left Professor Cromwell drying dishes for Emma while I crossed the road with Dora. Gazing out at a field pockmarked by platefuls of manure, I stood by the Allens' pasture gate, conjuring Roland— Roland driving the cows around the side of the barn at the end of the day, herding them in, strong and clear.

In Illinois, I had imagined Roland growing older, with children. I would have learned of it all from Emma and Dora. That the children weren't mine would sadden me, but at least he would be alive and prospering. Cold comfort. And, in the end, cold comfort finds a welcome.

This view from the pasture gate—the fields and trees, the cows, and, yes, the cowpats—seared me with longing. Dora stood on one side of me and then Emma on the other.

Dora opened the gate to let Red out into the pasture where he usually loved to menace the cows, lest they forget who was in charge. That he moved slowly and his tail hung listless was evidence of his own mourning.

As Dora closed the gate, Professor Cromwell, who must have been there some minutes, told me, "It's time."

# CHAPTER TWENTY-EIGHT

S weet Serena, you were with me still in late April 1919, though Denton was fading into ghosthood. Never forgotten, yet not quite present.

Our dream, Serena, of a gazebo and children playing tea party on a wide lawn beneath plane trees—I'd abandoned it with only a blown kiss of regret, for now I was home, leaning against the pasture gate of Roland's farm. Out where cattle nosed at still-cold and oozing ground for any grass, old or new, the trees nudged fledgling leaves into the world. The air was astringent, light and thin and pale yellow.

Beside me, Dora shifted. "Mountains of snow, tall as the barn eaves, covered the ground till the end of March," she said, gesturing toward the late April ponds that splotched the farther fields. "We'll be late planting."

Emma, at my other side, grunted concurrence, telling me, "We had to dig tunnels to the outhouse and henhouse and barns."

Pulling the old coat tight around me, I told Dora, "We'll need another hired man. Moses is tired. But God knows, he's been a good soldier."

"He says he'll scare up another hand. One as good as him, he says, though I doubt there is such a man," Dora said.

Following the sale of Aunt's house and furnishings on the first of March, I'd once again packed books, tea set, cowherd painting, and clothes into my old trunk. But before purchasing a railway ticket, I walked over to "little" Mrs. Pedersen's, explaining to her that I had lived in her house long ago.

"You're Mrs. Bullfinch's friend," she said. "Come in. Just wander around."

Mrs. Pedersen was given to quantities of tatting, crocheting, and cross-stitching, and to ladies' magazines and ceramic knick-knacks, many of them depicting praying children. Of Serena and Denton's presence nothing remained.

Later that day, I visited my parents' graves. Here again—beyond the quotes on their monuments—I found little of their presence. Now I was their vessel. At 4:12 p.m., I boarded the familiar train headed through Illinois, up into Iowa, and then home.

I settled into the room that had been Lily Allen's nursery. Despite the age of the house, this space retained the tangy, homely odor of raw wood. And, indeed, the pine floor would need paint and a rug. Outside the window stood the rock elm, in bud, to shade and shelter me even as it had Roland.

I hung the painting of the flaxen-haired cowherd above a bedside bookcase hauled home from the secondhand store in Harvester, along with a small writing desk at which I could corresponded with Beardsley friends. On a later trip to town, I haggled for yet another bookcase, this one for the parlor.

Atop the bedside shelves were the china tea set and the

photograph of Serena and Denton, beginning to fade a little. Owing perhaps to her own lack of family, Dora had adopted mine as aunt and uncle. Recently she—now a devoted Methodist—concluded mealtime grace with, "Lord, look after Aunt Serena and Uncle Denton in heaven."

Myself, I still imagined Serena and Denton living in a big white house set back from the street, where plane trees shade the lawn. In the gazebo, come late afternoon, Serena pours tea.

The upper bookcase shelves held Serena's books. Hidden in *The Return of the Native* was the note Roland had written me, as was the one I had written him, the one Dora found and I later pilfered. His photograph I secreted in *Leaves of Grass*. On the bottom shelf were sent-away-for books: *Cradles of Civilization* and *Aristotle and Alexander of Macedon*.

One day, standing at the stove, Dora said, "One time I wondered if it was you that Roland loved. Isn't that strange? Your name doesn't start with *B*." She gave a little laugh and stirred the gravy. My pulse stumbled, but I was so hungry to hear his name spoken aloud that I welcomed her random thoughts.

Beside me at the table, the ghost of Roland shook his head in wonderment.


Yesterday, the mailbox at the Harvester post office held an unexpected letter from Professor Cromwell. The two and a half months after Roland's funeral, culminating in the professor's departure from Beardsley, had been vexatious and disheartening. I had finally told him the truth on the train, and as a result he'd stopped coming to the house or noticing me in the college halls. Now he had written, beginning with a breezy "The Pittsburgh laboratory is everything I could hope for, and I have settled in without a hitch."

But he went on to say, "Often I ponder your words on the train from Harvester to Beardsley. You said I was in love with Serena, not you. I was angry that you doubted my feelings, and bitter that you didn't return them. I behaved badly and I regret that.

"With the passage of years (can it be nine?) since Serena and Denton's deaths, it grows less painful to look back on the good times we enjoyed. I confess that I loved them both, though in different ways, of course."

In *what* ways, Barrett?

He went on: "It is freeing to acknowledge this. And as a man who was never meant to live out his years without a helpmeet, maybe I'm ready to begin the search for the woman who'll have me.

"On another topic, I do not and never will understand the romance of the agrarian life—the unremitting labor, the nauseating odors, the failed crops. Still, here we are! We're quite different people.

"I realized that I had lost you when I saw you in your setting—the two farms. It was clear then that you could never accept my proposal, though, foolishly, I had to pursue it. Nothing ventured . . .

"Having said all this, I still hold, as I said on the train, that Roland Allen was an adolescent infatuation. You were only a girl. You will recover."

The letter smacked of male pride and of sadness too. I could be magnanimous. Except for Roland, I had all that I wanted.

And though Roland was gone—the one I would lie with in dreams—his ghost came looking for me when I walked to the lake or sat smoking on the back stoop. Always I ran to him and always my embraces came away empty. I stored his visits in the tapestry bag with a shiny brass closing, and knew I would never leave this place so long as his shadow endured. At night, one side of the bed remained undisturbed, waiting.

Odd to say, I often thought of Aunt. Though she had been un-repentant, she'd also been a soul in torment. I wished her peace in her Jesus marriage. We had both loved heedlessly. Did I de-serve my happiness, I wondered in odd moments, immediately thrusting the thought away. I had no time for Jesuitical specula-tion. Too much work waited for me.

In the chill of this April morning, from across the pasture, a huge Percheron named Montana came walking toward us, his pace leisurely, his head bobbing yes as he came. Legs splayed across the broad back of the horse, Roland yearned toward us, evanescing as Montana drew near the gate and offered his head to be petted.

Emma reached out to the horse, asking Dora, "Where do things stand with the bank?" Only Emma could come right out like that, inquiring the way a sister would.

"We're pretty near square," Dora told her. "Ruby paid off the tractor with some of her house money. She even bought a couple of decent chairs for the parlor." She lifted her chin. "We're look-ing civilized and solvent. That's what Ruby says."

Emma nodded. "This is gonna work." She caressed the horse's ears. "It's gonna work."

And it has worked, through these ensuing decades since my return. We are growing older, Dora and I—I'll be forty-seven. Dora, still childlike, will be fifty. Our faces are seamed and spare.

Across Cemetery Road, dear Emma is seventy-five and thriv-ing, farming over seven hundred acres with the boys and a hired man. She drives a 1941 Buick that Henry purchased shortly be-fore his death the day after Pearl Harbor.

Because Emma is a widow with a farm to run and because farms are necessary to the war effort, Dan and Sol have hardship deferrals from military service. Though they can see the necessity, they've taken it hard not to fight the Axis. Sol says, "If we could get a couple more men out here to work, we could still go."

Barrett Cromwell has an important wartime appointment in the Roosevelt administration, something hush-hush. He never found a helpmeet: he remains married to his work.

As for me, well, last week, while I walked down a row of young corn, I was seized by such happiness I had to stoop and pinch crumbs of black dirt between my fingers, tasting them in my mouth. The soil in St. Bridget County is, I'm told, among the most fertile in the world.

Since I moved in with Dora, the two of us have been objects of speculation in Harvester. Early days, Emma set folks straight on the question of whether our relationship was a romantic one. That settled, people, women especially, wondered why we never sought marriage.

"That's hard work, that farming. Why'd a woman want to do all that heavy lifting and hauling? Donald tells me he's seen 'em throwing those bales around like any man. You see the muscles they've got? I'm not sure it's womanly." Emma had heard this in Sue's Beauty Parlor while she was having her hair permed.

"Well, I don't know," Sue had said. "The money they make is theirs to do with, no man taking it or telling them it's for the new Ford. Doesn't sound so bad to me." Some nodding of heads followed this.

"Think they'll ever move to town?" Town people assumed that this was the goal of every farmer.

"No," Sue said, "The dark one—the one with all the words— told me she'd never get the dirt out from under her fingernails."

Someone, Emma perhaps, said that my vocabulary was often remarked on. Was I trying to be high-hat, or was I some kind of genius? And if I was some kind of genius, what was I doing on the farm?

I never passed up an opportunity to provide village entertainment, scattering "autodidact," "*je ne sais quoi*," and "antediluvian" in my path as I went. I'd have disappointed had I not.

After a couple of decades, Dora and I have been accepted, I think, with a certain fondness as Harvester's own lady eccentrics.

Even now, Dora continues to tack addendum onto grace. Recently it was: "And thank you, God, for sending me a sister."

And we *have* been sisters, in ways that she'll never know. But more obviously, as sisters, we have hung onto Roland's farm through two depressions, even adding acreage. We're thrifty. We kept the wagon and horses well into the thirties, then bought a secondhand Ford and a new tractor from old Kolchak when the one that killed Roland died. We still keep it as a kind of memorial. Each spring I drag out red paint and give it a fresh coat, singing the old forbidden words as I work.

Dora is not, for the most part, a thinker, but to this day she ponders the identity of Roland's lover. When we go to town on Saturdays, she tells me, she studies the women our age. The woman in the next booth at the Loon Cafe who dyes her hair, is she the one? Or the redhead behind the counter in Lundeen's Dry Goods?

In payment for my transgression and her endless speculation, I am the best of sisters to her. But in truth, I am no better when it comes to speculation. While some wrestle with the meaning of life or the existence of God, I wrestle with the meaning of Roland's message: *I live on hope.* In bed at night or kneeling in the garden, I consider the words as they might have applied to the two of us. Did he imagine that I would return? Or was he planning to leave Dora when the debts were paid?

Does everyone have a mystery they tease in this manner, after all hope of an answer is dead? What strange stubborn creatures we are, forever worrying a hangnail.

If Roland's ghost could talk, perhaps he'd explain. *I live on hope.* But as it is, he comes to me silent, a large black dog loping at his side. I open my arms to them.

Leila Navidi

FAITH SULLIVAN is the author of many novels, including *Gardenias*, *The Cape Ann*, *What a Woman Must Do*, and, most recently, *Good Night, Mr. Wodehouse*. A "demon gardener, flea marketer, and feeder of birds," she is also an indefatigable champion of literary culture and her fellow writers, and has visited with hundreds of book clubs. Born and raised in southern Minnesota, she spent twenty-some years in New York and Los Angeles, but now lives in Minneapolis with her husband.

milkweed
editions

Founded as a nonprofit organization in 1980,
Milkweed Editions is an independent publisher. Our mission is
to identify, nurture and publish transformative literature,
and build an engaged community around it.

We are aided in this mission by generous individuals who make
a gift to underwrite books on our list. Special underwriting for
*Ruby & Roland* was provided anonymously.

milkweed.org

Interior design by Mary Austin Speaker
Typeset in Bulmer

Bulmer was designed by William Martin in 1792 for printing
the Boydell Shakespeare folio edition. Bulmer is a late transi-
tional typeface that offered a British response to the delicate
Italian type work of the Italian and French type foundries of
Bodoni and Didot.